D1175832

Wildfire

Also by Carrie Mac

10 Things I Can See from Here

Wildfire

Carrie Mac

ALFRED A. KNOPF
New York

THIS IS A BORZOI BOOK PUBLISHED BY ALFRED A. KNOPF

Visit us on the Web! GetUnderlined.com

Educators and librarians, for a variety of teaching tools, visit us at
RHTeachersLibrarians.com

Library of Congress Cataloging-in-Publication Data
Names: Mac, Carrie, author.
Title: Wildfire / Carrie Mac.
Description: First edition. | New York: Alfred A. Knopf, 2020. |
Summary: Teenaged best friends Annie and Pete go on a backpacking trip
in the Pacific Northwest, with dangerous consequences.
Identifiers: LCCN 2018058307 (print) | LCCN 2018060469 (ebook) |
ISBN 978-0-399-55631-9 (ebook) | ISBN 978-0-399-55629-6 (trade) |
ISBN 978-0-399-55630-2 (lib. bdg.)
Subjects: | CYAC: Best friends—Fiction. | Friendship—Fiction. | Wildfires—Fiction. |
Fires—Fiction. | Survival—Fiction. | Wilderness areas—Fiction.
Classification: LCC PZ7.M111845 (ebook) | LCC PZ7.M111845 Wi 2020 (print) |
DDC [Fic]—dc23

The text of this book is set in 11-point Berling LT Std.
Interior design by Cathy Bobak

Printed in the United States of America
January 2020
10 9 8 7 6 5 4 3 2 1
First Edition

For Hawk

Ace fire starter, fellow stargazer, my sun

✧ ✧ ✧

You and me were always with each other
Before we knew the other was ever there
You and me, we belong together
Just like a breath needs the air.

—Alecia Moore and Dallas Green

Red Twilight

JUNE 26

I am cradling Pete's head in my lap, sitting by the tent flap, looking out. Wildfires are closing in from the west and the south, with smoke so thick it's like a bank of fog across the whole sky, turning the sun, which is just about to slip behind the mountain, into a blood-orange ball. In this strange twilight, everything looks like it's been washed in thin blue shadows. Even Pete. He looked so red in the daylight, because of the fever, but also because of the orange nylon of the tent he has not been out of since yesterday. The air in here smells like sour milk and the rankest body odor you can imagine. Not Pete's regular body odor, which I once described to him as skunk cabbage and cinnamon stew, with a dollop of sour cream past its best-by date on top. Call me weird, but I never minded it. But this is different. Not quite like how Gigi smelled with the lung cancer chewing her up from the inside out, but similar. Dangerously sour. Uniquely foul. Scary, if a smell can actually make you afraid.

I close my eyes and will something beautiful to take over, something to make this moment simple and quiet and dim and safe. Gigi, her hair in rollers, sitting on the back porch in her sateen dressing gown with the peacocks on it, painting her nails while I shuck a bowl of Dad's peas, sweet and plump. The sun just about setting, and Gigi telling me why she thinks Robert Redford is the man she should've married. My mom playing the piano inside. Pete climbing that slant of rock a few days ago, and me, with my bare feet on the hot dirt, looking up at him and the blue sky beyond. That was the last time we saw blue sky. He let go with his right hand and reached up. I wish I'd taken a picture of that one moment, when he looked like he was about to scoop up a handful of sky and drink it. I don't need more pictures of the two of us, like the ones we did take. I need pictures of him. Just Pete.

It's almost dark enough to use my headlamp, but I'm not going to waste the battery. Outside the flap, I watch the moon rising so slowly.

"It looks like a werewolf movie just before the transformation," I say. "What's that one Gigi loved?" I know what it is, but I hope he'll say it. Or say anything. He hasn't said a word for too many hours to think about. I give him what feels like the longest time to think of it and say it, but he doesn't. *"American Werewolf in London,"* I say. "That's the one."

He nods, a tiny smile on his lips.

"She was definitely not a movie snob," I say with a little

laugh. "Remember when she took us to see *Children of the Corn* that Halloween? How old were we? Way too young. That scene right at the beginning in Hanzer's Coffee Shop, when the kids poison the coffee and then murder all the adults? They stick that one guy's hand in the meat slicer? We were only eleven."

He shakes his head and barely lifts both hands, fingers splayed.

"Ten?" Right. Just a few months after his mom died. "Way too soon, right?"

He nods.

"She knew it," I say. "Or else she wouldn't have told us not to tell the dads."

I wish we were actually having a conversation about Gigi's obsession with Hollywood, and not here wondering if the fires are going to close in on us. Like this tent, which is closing in on us.

We bought this tent after almost a year of walking dogs, when we were fourteen. It weighs only as much as three blocks of butter, but we can sit up in it and play cards and drink cheap powdered hot chocolate we buy in bulk at Thrifty Mart. It's a very, very tight fit, especially considering that Pete grew three inches after we bought it. Gigi said that he grew three inches the *day* after we bought it, but the truth is that we bought it on Black Friday, and then we didn't use it until spring break, so I guess no one should've been surprised, considering Pete was as tall as his dad by the time we were thirteen. That's when Gigi put a mark above all the others on the doorway where my dad has been tracking our heights. She used permanent marker and wrote the date of his sixteenth birthday. Her prediction, she said. She was absolutely right.

Right now this tent feels like a coffin.

We have to get out.

"*American Werewolf in London* was a bad one to bring up," I say. "Sorry." Best friends backpacking, attacked by a pack of wolves. One is mauled to death, one becomes a werewolf.

"You be the werewolf," Pete murmurs.

"Pete!" I hold his cheeks in my hands. "Hi!"

He opens his eye just for a few seconds, and I really get to see him, because otherwise he doesn't look like himself. His forehead is slick with sweat, and his puffy cheeks are red and shiny with oil. I can't look at his nose, or lips, or ears, which are black at the tips and getting worse. Look at his necklace instead, Annie. An instant of panic sends my fingers to find the matching one around my neck. It's still there, thankfully. If I lose mine, or he loses his, things will only get worse. This is very hard to imagine. We need all the serendipity, magic, and luck we can muster. God too, if it's a believing sort of day. I touch his necklace with one hand and mine with the other.

I believe in the talismans that I keep in a bulging Altoids tin, so many tiny pieces of the planet that Pete and I have found. I believe that if Pete has them, everything might end up better than if he didn't have them. Not to say that I think they will fix this. I just know that they won't make it any worse. I shake out his filthy, sweat-soaked sleeping bag, which I should've laid out on a rock to air, and move aside mine too. I don't see the tin.

Pete lifts a hand to show me that he has it, bulging with luck and good fortune and all things wishes-come-true. There is so much good luck in there that I am absolutely certain something, something, *something* good is going to happen. A plane overhead. A fire crew within earshot of the whistle I sound as often as I think to. Enough rest and water and PowerGels that Pete gets strong enough to walk out of here, or I develop the superhuman strength that moms get when they have to lift a car off their child with their own bare hands. I need that strength, to carry Pete out of here on my own.

"Show me," Pete says as he hands me the tin.

I pull off the elastic band that keeps it from popping open because it's so full. That's how much good luck is in there.

Inside, on top, a small, clear, perfectly faceted crystal. I hold it up to the light. It seems impossible that it came out of the earth, and we found it just days ago, when nothing was wrong yet. When we were digging in the dirt like two little kids, putting our treasures into plastic beach buckets.

"Where did you get that?" he says.

"You know, Pete."

"Tell me, though." His words are thick and slow. "Each one. Story."

We've been through the tin twice.

The last time was only an hour ago, when the sun was still up but slanting toward the end of the day.

Pete's wearing his favorite shirt, soft and thin, dark blue with a silver unicorn leaping over a silver mountain, with a silver moon overhead. It is caked in vomit, though, and so wet with sweat that I could wring it out. His body is trying to fix this, and for days I had absolute faith that it would, but now I'm restless with dread. I can't leave him, and I can't stay. If I go, he'll be alone. If I stay, there will be no help. I have rocks spelling "SOS" by the creek, in the clearing. I was sure that one of the water bombers would've seen it by now. That was my Big Plan, and it hasn't worked. Neither did setting signal fires. A triangle of three, which means "help." But no surprise that one more little fire gets ignored when half the state is on fire.

Right now I'll take him outside. He can get some fresh air—smoky, yes, but better than the heady air in the tent. He can feel the breeze on his wet face, let his sweaty and impossibly swollen, red body feel the world outside this tent, even if it's burning to the ground out there. And maybe I can think just a little bit better.

"Let's go outside," I say. "Get some air. Do us both good."

He nods.

"I hate it in here," he whispers in a slur. "Like a coffin."

"Let's get you out, then." I close up the tin without the band and give it back to him. "Hold that for a sec."

He nods again, fingers tightening around it.

"I'm going to slide you," I say. "Fast or slow?"

"Fast."

"Good choice." I ease his head off my lap and onto the makeshift pillow of clothes folded into his hoodie. I shift him over so he's centered on the sleeping mat. He's lying on his thin quick-dry towel, and I am so grateful that we decided to bring those; otherwise, he'd be sticking to the foam because it's been too hot even to lie on the sleeping bag since late morning. He grunts a little, but I keep working. I clear the things away from the door of the tent. Our headlamps, the pot and pocket stove, the Uno cards we haven't touched for a couple of days.

"Outside will help so much, Pete. I saw a few bats last night. And an owl. You can really hear them in this valley. Maybe we'll even hear some wolves, which would be awesome, so long as they stay way the hell away from us. Maybe coyotes instead. Yeah, that'd be better. Just little scrawny coyotes yipping."

He grunts.

"Hang on," I say as I take hold of the foot of his sleeping bag. I shimmy him down to the vestibule as gently as I can. This is not fresh air at all, but it's better than being in the tent. I stand up, my muscles aching from having sat on the hard ground for so long, my legs so wobbly that I have to take an extra few seconds to get solid footing before I use my feet to clear a path through the pebbles and pinecones and sticks. Don't stop, Annie. This is *doing* something. I turn back to the tent and see that Pete is moving.

"Stay still, dumb-ass," I say. "Give me a sec. I'm going to pull you all the way out, but not over a bunch of rocks."

But then I realize that he's having a seizure. Not a huge one like you see in movies, but as if someone turned the dial down on one like that. Without thinking, I reach in and grab the foam mat and yank him out in one incredible pull. Three steps and he's clear of the tent. He is a foot taller and fifty pounds heavier than me, but he feels as light as a little kid. I grab his shoulder and far knee and pull him onto his side, like the home nurse showed me to do with Gigi when she started to have trouble swallowing but was still eating mashed everything.

"Stop it, Pete." I hold him from tipping right over, his entire body stiff and shaking, his legs kicking at nothing, his eyes wide open and staring at me without seeing me at all. "Stop it."

I should've been counting.

"Stop it, Pete! Stop it! Stop it! Stop it!"

How long has this been happening? What about when I wasn't looking? Is this it? Is he dying? Right now?

I lift my eyes up and whisper to the god that I don't believe in but wish I did.

"Please make him okay. Please, *please* make him better. Please tell me what to do."

When he is finally still, he doesn't say anything. He just breathes, shallow and fast. I squat beside him and watch him for a long time, waiting for another seizure. When my knees buckle, I lie down beside him, my head on my arm, the cool dirt and pebbles under me. He's better now. I can close my eyes for just a second, like an amen.

I am sure that I don't sleep, but it is dusk when I open my eyes, and so much cooler. I know I must've dozed off, my arms around him. Something is different on the horizon, along the ridge of low-slung mountains to the west, where the sun is just disappearing. It's like it's actually touching down on the forest, because there is a gossamer thread of rippling orange flames, the air above it giving up and melting into a watery wash of heat.

Pete is asleep. This is good.

The little tin full of good luck and good fortune and hope and beautiful things and tiny treasures lies open on the ground, the talismans scattered on the dirt.

I lean forward, about to let go of Pete to collect all the shiny bits of hope from the hot, dry forest floor, where they are lost under pine needles and debris. I squint, and realize that I can see only some of them in the hazy moonlight. If I want to go get them, I have to let go of Pete. I can't do that.

My talismans are still good luck, I tell myself. Even if they are scattered on the dirt in the wilderness. They are my good luck, and so I get to say that they can still be good luck if they're lost.

But I don't really believe that they are lucky anymore, because this has been the unluckiest time of all.

This might even be the way that we actually die, with no

one left behind to write the tragic event in the Notebook of Doom. When we get home, I will write ten pages about this. At least.

For now, I don't want Pete to wake and see how close the wildfire is, so I grab the mat this time and pull him back into the tent. That will be more comfortable.

He opens his eyes but quickly closes them again.

"Do you know what day it is, Pete?"

"Wednesday."

"Correct," I say. "What grade did I get in biology?"

"Trick question." He's speaking so quietly that I have to be nearly cheek to cheek to hear him. "You failed. Not just biology. The whole year."

"Who is the president?"

"Annie," Pete says. "Why are you asking this stuff?"

"You had a seizure. Aren't you supposed to ask questions like that?"

"A seizure?" Pete struggles to sit up. "That's crazy."

"Exactly." I help him take a drink from the pot of water.

"I feel a bit better now."

"Maybe it was your fever breaking."

"Maybe." He starts to roll onto his knees. "I'm going to go take a leak."

"No!" I grab his arm. "Just use this." I hand him the bag. "I'll go out. You're not strong enough yet."

I leave him inside and go out by myself. I stand right in front of the tent in case he tries to look out. He cannot see what I'm seeing. The flames are taller now, wicking along the tops of trees just across the valley. The moon is red. The smoke is thick and drifting our way.

This is a terrible place to be.

We have to get out of here.

Notebook of Doom

My printing on the cover was done with marker, but not indelible marker, so the words are mostly smeared. The book is a flipbook that was in Pete's stocking one year. Flip it one way and you see a unicorn jumping over a happy-face sun. Flip it the other way and the unicorn is jumping over a sleeping moon. It is a very cute book, considering the peril that lies within.

NOTEBOOK OF DOOM: A CHRONICLE OF STUPID STUNTS AND/OR NEAR-DEATH EXPERIENCES
By Annie Banana Poltava and Unicorn Pete Bonner

Bullet in the brain (age 8)
We took the BB gun to our fort at Otis Creek, even though Annie's dad said Always Have Him Help. But he moved to Bellingham, and so he was not around to Have Him Help, and Annie's mom didn't know that

we took it and a bag of Pete's dad's beer cans with us after school. We filled the old Pabst cans with water and lined them up on a log. Annie was about to pull the trigger when a dumb pheasant flapped right in her line of sight, and so she swung the gun out of the way and squeezed the trigger at the same time and with one *phsst* a pellet shot straight into the middle of Pete's forehead.

Once we realized that Pete wasn't dying, we wiped it with alcohol and put a Band-Aid on it and told our parents (except for Annie's dad) that he fell at the creek.

The pellet is still in there, as far as we know.

Bee sting (age 11)
We camped overnight at our fort for the Very First Time. The dads told us not to have a fire, but we did because it was cold by the creek and we'd brought marshmallows. Marshmallows = fire. We started the fire again in the morning, to have the other half of the bag. Pete was adding little twigs to get it going while Annie took down the tent. When she didn't come after a long while, he went to look for her and found her kneeling on the ground, about to tip over, clutching her throat.

"Bee!" she croaked.

"Bee!" he hollered while he dumped her backpack and did not find the EpiPen she was supposed to carry with her. "Bee!" He dumped his pack too and found the backup EpiPen Annie's dad had given him.

"Bee!" he yelled again as he swiftly and heroically stabbed her with it.

She recovered, and we hiked home and got there in time. We never told about the fire we'd had at Otis Creek, or the bee sting, most of all. We ripped Annie's room apart and found the pen behind her dresser and then told her dad that she'd lost it, just so we'd both have one from then on. Annie could easily admit that not being able to breathe is a very bad thing.

Fall from a height (age 13)

Annie bet Pete that she could jump off the Sparkle Clean Laundry's roof and tuck into a roll, parkour-style, thus dissipating the impact. She landed flat on her back somehow, her breath punched out of her with so much force that Pete thought everything had exploded inside her and her brains would start leaking out of her ears. She lay there for a long time. Not moving, eyes closed, breathing shallow. Pete still maintains that Annie was actually dead for a couple of seconds at least. Annie claims that she was trying to add a flip, and could've if she'd jumped from a little higher.

Don't argue with the ocean (age 15)

We read the timetables wrong coming back from hiking to Liberty Cove. Annie's dad dropped us off to camp for two nights, and we were due back at the parking lot to get picked up by Pete's dad. We had to cross the little cove, which was engulfed by a gigantic and steady swell. We'd have to jump. Was it ten feet maybe? More or less. Annie had no doubt she could make it. She said she'd go first. She landed in the water.

"Swim!" Pete jumped in after her as a wave crested overhead.

Our packs filled with water, pulling us under. It was cold. Annie hit her head on something. Pete reached for her, but we were yanked apart by the waves rolling back. Neither of us tried to wrestle out of our pack, which was entirely stupid. But can you imagine how much it would cost to replace all our gear? Death versus a few hundred dollars to replace our gear off Craigslist. Duh. We both sank to the ocean floor. There was Pete, his eyes squeezed shut. Annie didn't have any breath left. Then, as if the ocean had made a very clear and somewhat angry conclusion, a huge wave lifted us up and pushed us toward the beach, dumping us on a carpet of sharp rock. We dragged our packs and ourselves to the parking lot, which was just over the dune. Pete's dad was nowhere in sight, and even though our phones were in a dry bag, there was no signal. By the time he showed up, we'd mostly dried off in the sun but still had to explain why our gear was soaking wet.

We told him the truth, because Everett can appreciate a story like that. He figures if it ends well, then every other bad decision gets a pass.

But don't tell Annie's dad, he said. Which we had no plan to do anyway.

Annie wants the following stated for the official record: I could have made it if I had a running start.

Pete wants the following stated for the official record: There are no running starts on boulders.

The black dog (age 16)

The day Gigi's doctor said there was nothing else they could do.

"Except for hospice," she said. "There is a spot in Bellingham. It's beautiful. A little cottage at the edge of a park with hundreds of rhododendron bushes that are just about to bloom."

"Each one of those blooms can kiss my ass," Gigi whispered, her eyes closed against the constant pain. "They're only going to die too."

The doctor glanced at Annie, then her father.

"She's coming home," her dad said.

"She's coming home," Annie said.

"What they said," Gigi said.

"We'll make you as comfortable as we can." The doctor put her hand on Gigi's knee. "If that's what you want."

That night, while Gigi solidly slept, wheezing wetly,

Annie sat on the edge of the bed, holding her hand, Gigi's skeletal fingers tipped with her fresh manicure—"I'll die with Fatal Attraction Red on my nails and a tiny rhinestone set in each one." Gigi's booze cabinet and mini fridge were right there, so Annie made a vodka and 7UP for Gigi and one for herself and drank both while trucks scooped up people in *Soylent Green*, playing on mute behind her. Then another drink. And one more, because what did anything matter if Gigi was going to die, *soon*? And then she went out the back door with the car keys and got into the car to drive to Pete's—even though it was only a few blocks away—but instead of turning onto his street, she hit the telephone pole, slamming to a stop, the airbag exploding in her face and cracking her wrist. She called Pete and then passed out. He dialed 911 as he ran. He is not ashamed to admit that he was bawling as he approached the mangled car. He is also not ashamed to admit that he bawled even more when she seemed to be mostly okay, thanks to the airbags deployed on three sides.

"You braked for a dog," Pete said as the sirens got louder and louder. "You saw a dog in the road and you couldn't stop in time, and so you hit the pole. A black dog that was hard to see at first, Banana. No vodka. You're just upset because of your grandma."

Annie was nodding, holding the wrist that Pete had tucked into the folded blanket she always kept on the backseat. That was easy. She *was* upset because of Gigi.

She told the paramedics about the dog. She told the nurses. Her father. Pete's father. She told Gigi when she called her to tell her that her wrist was broken and she was fine and to *rest and do not come* because she'd be home in a couple of hours. She told the X-ray technician. It was a Lab, she said. Black Lab, which was why it was so hard to see it. By the time she told the young doctor about the dog, she nearly believed it was true. There had been a dog. Black as night. Slam the brakes. And then the crash.

The doctor rolled his eyes, and when it was only Pete and Annie with curtains drawn all around, he said that he wouldn't tell her dad because he believed in second chances, which was either a very nice thing to do for her or a very stupid thing. Annie votes nice thing. Pete votes very stupid thing.

There are two other near-deaths listed in that book, but Pete and I never wrote the stories, mostly just in case the dads read them. Or Gigi. We keep them at the back of the book, where the unicorn and sleepy moon are. Maybe when we're grown-ups, we'll write about them then.

Drowning at Lake Shannon (age 11)
That time we were kidnapped (age 12)

The Dying Process

MAY 8

Before that horrible sunset on the mountain with Pete, before Gigi died, we left the doctor's office with her for the last time. After that half hour with the doctor, Dad, Gigi, Pete, and I had more knowledge about the Death with Dignity Act than we could ever use. Considering none of us had ever heard about it before, it was a lot of information all at once.

The last thing the doctor did before we left was lean forward and put her hand on Gigi's knee.

"I must be clear. You are now in the dying process," she said. "It will not get better. I cannot fix this. I know that you understand, but your family must too."

None of us said anything until we got into the car.

"Why didn't you tell us?" I asked, but as soon as the words were out of my mouth, I knew why. Gigi and the doctor had already had this discussion. Gigi already knew that once a dying person decided to stop eating and drinking, you did not offer so much as a sip of water, even on the days into the final slide toward a starving, parched demise.

"Why didn't you tell us about this?" I pressed the pamphlet to her bony chest. She held it there, not looking at it because she already knew what it said.

"The time is right," she whispered through a throat lined with tiny glass shards. She didn't tell me that's what it felt like to swallow, but I read it in her notebook, where she'd filled dozens of pages with notes and words for what she called "Death's Wardrobe."

I can't say anything about what I read. Because we have an agreement in our house. Her, me, and Dad. No one reads the personal stuff.

"I will be like a good poem," Gigi said. "It's all about the denouement."

"How can you even say that?" I started to cry.

It could not be fixed.

You cannot fix a dead person. Both Pete and I know that. We've been the two sole members of the Dead Mom Club since we were twelve. Pete was the only member of the club before that. His mom died when we were ten. It's not that it was only ever supposed to be the two of us, but none of the other kids' mothers have died since then. It doesn't happen all that often. It's a very small club.

I crashed the car that night. Avoiding the black dog. Gigi came with my dad to the hospital, even though I begged her to stay home. She appeared at my bedside when Pete was stalking the vending machines and my dad was dealing with an insurance glitch. Her portable oxygen tank hung heavy off of one shoulder, making her lean awkwardly on her two canes—one sparkly blue, one baby pink with tiny red hearts all over it—and all my guts twisted into a ball. I'd made her get up in the middle of the night, when she should be peacefully getting on with the not-very-peaceful parts of dying.

She sat beside me on the bed. "When one is trying to dramatically die with as much Hollywood glamour as something so wretched can include, beauty sleep is absolutely essential. The good doctor did say so, didn't she? Just this afternoon?"

"She did not."

"Then it must be in the pamphlet." Gigi took it out of her purse and tried to give it to me.

"I don't want it." I wished I'd never read it. It was basically instructions for how to starve to death. It even said that you could expect your loved one to have sweet breath just before they died.

"Right under 'Your Life, Your Death, Your Choice.' "

"This isn't funny, Gigi," I said. "I am a spoiled brat. And I am so, so sorry. I wasn't thinking. This is the last thing you need—"

"Maybe it's under 'Palliative Needs.' "

"This is not funny!" Then came the tears. I hadn't cried in the car, the crash, the ambulance, or the ER. "I miss you already and you're not even dead yet!"

She pulled me into the lightest hug, like it was the ghost

of her wrapping those thin, pale arms around me, and not the woman I genuinely believed could leap tall buildings if she wanted to.

"You can't make this better," she said. "And I can't keep coming to get you. Not anymore, Annie. This is going to be about me. From now until the end. When I'm gone, you can be as dysfunctional as you want, but please know that you are smarter than that. And that I've given Pete instructions to protect you from yourself, if required."

"She has," Pete said from the doorway, arms full of vending machine junk, and a ginger ale for Gigi, to go with the two little vodka bottles in her purse.

"Until then, this is mine to finish," Gigi said. "And yours to help. Understood?"

"Yes, Gigi."

"Good girl. Pete?"

"Yes, ma'am."

"Good, good. Yay for death. Now for some arts and crafts, which works as a therapeutic distraction for little kids, and so there is no reason why it can't help us now." She reached into her purse and pulled out a rainbow of permanent markers secured with an elastic band. She took my brand-new cast in her bony hands, rested it on a pillow in her lap, and started drawing flowers.

"Dying doesn't make me a better artist," she said. "I can write a beautiful poem, but I'll save that for a sealed envelope in my bedside drawer with your name written on it to read after I die."

I waited a moment to say it, because I was trying to decide if she was serious. She beat me to it, smiling up at me with a yellow-toothed grin and wrinkles like little drapes hung at the edges of her mouth.

"There won't be a poem," she said in the quiet, hoarse voice that seemed to be getting quieter by the day. She drew another black outline of a flower and started to color it in. "You know it takes me twenty years to write a good one. And I refuse to leave you a piece of crap. What a terrible legacy that would be."

That was the last time she left the house. Four weeks later, she was dead.

Atrophy

JUNE 17

The colorful flowers on the cast are still vibrant, even if the cast is beat-up and was supposed to come off yesterday. I can almost slip it off, but I haven't demonstrated that to anyone. I think if I just wait another week or two, my arm will have atrophied so much that the cast will slip right off and I won't have to cut through the flower garden Gigi drew all over it. She didn't even leave a square inch for Pete, so he found the flower with the biggest center and signed his initials there. He also found a spot of foliage and drew a unicorn horn, and the tiniest bit of a unicorn head, so it looked like it was either peeking out all nymphish and coy or being smothered by a witch's spell of so many flowers that there was nowhere to breathe, even if there were so many places to hide.

Most of me knows that letting my muscles perish for even one day more is stupid, when one of the things I am most looking forward to is rock climbing at Ugly Mug with Pete.

And Preet too, I suppose. It might help if I could imagine Gigi saying, *Don't be silly, darling, it's just a cast.* Except what she would really say is, *It would make quite the souvenir from your dead, dead Gigi. Maybe you could turn it into a lamp. What a conversation piece.*

I knew that the right thing to do was to go get it cut off. And so even without Pete—because I was still me without him!—I was going to do it. Right, Gigi? I'm still me without him. I don't need him for *everything.*

But isn't it wonderful to have such a divine connection with another person. You and Pete are symbiotic, darling. Enjoy it.

Not helpful, Gigi.

I told Pete that he didn't need to come, because I wanted to show Gigi that I could do it by myself. Actually, that's not accurate. I knew that Preet was being awarded a big scholarship by the Poppen Future Lawyer Foundation in Seattle, and I didn't want to make Pete choose, because then he would've launched into his *But what do I do? Who do I choose?* angst and I didn't want that. If I'd told him, he'd have wanted to come with me, even though he'd already promised to go with Preet. So I didn't say anything, because I don't want to be that best friend who wields ten years over a paltry few months. And! AND the biggest reason is because I can do it myself.

I told Pete I'd send pictures of the slaughter. I told my dad not to worry, I'd be fine, and asked if he wanted something from the Bear Claw Bakery on the way back. But then I just didn't go. I didn't make the turn. I didn't drive down the highway. I just pulled over and stared at the flowers on my cast, and thought about how I did not want the doctor sawing through them. Not yet. Not ever, to be honest.

I wanted to make a lamp. I would shellac the hell out of that thing and turn it into a frigging bedside lamp. *Don't you mean chandelier, darling?*

Right here is where I could say that I got out of the car and drank in the grounding majesty of the mountains towering all around. The truth, however, is that I started laughing. Mildly at first, then cackling and howling so hard that I was crying. Sad tears and funny tears and all of them turning my face into a wet, blotchy mess. I kept my hands on the wheel and my eyes locked on those claustrophobic mountains and prayed no police officer would ask me why I was pulled over on the shoulder.

Screw it. I got out and flapped my arms and tried to stop crying, but that just made my cast slide up and down and hit my wrist over and over. These mountains are not claustrophobic. Not to me. My mother hated them, and wrote entire compositions about their dark powers.

Not me.

These are my mountains.

It was a clear day, but the tops of the mountains were shrouded in a smoky haze. It was starting already. Or, more accurately, wildfires had been popping up and being put out for weeks, but there hadn't been that much smoke until now.

Now there were fires that couldn't be contained. Burning and burning despite every effort to put them out. Carrying on, arrogant and sure of their hunger, of the wilderness they wanted to eat. Just before I'd left the house, Pete had texted me from the event that this smoke was from a fire on the west side of Ross Lake.

Let the wildfire season begin! Good luck at the doc. Countdown to Fire Camp!

I started to text him back, but I couldn't find the right words.

About Fire Camp. I don't think I'm going to go, but you

Delete.

Wait, a fire on the west side of Ross Lake? Plus this wind? That meant I should smell it. Did I? I started again.

Did you smell it? I don't smell anything. Must be small.

His reply was immediate:

500-acre burn area. More later, going into ceremony. Make sure doc doesn't cut off your arm. You need it for camp.

For Fire Camp. "Where Future Wildfire Fighters Learn to Fight!" Pete and I had worked on my dad for the last three summers just to get him to agree to let me go when we were old enough. Ultimately, he still doesn't want me to go, but he's wisely decided not to stop me.

"Do you know what 'self-immolation' means?" he asked as he held a pen over the place where he had to sign his permission.

"Okay, that's really grim and you should be ashamed for exposing your vulnerable young child to such horrors. Also,

Fire Camp is not the same as dousing myself with gas and lighting a match, Dad."

"Isn't it, though?" He was grinning because he was trying to be funny, but I know him better than that. Funny doesn't work well for him. He's the kind of guy who goes to make a toast at a municipal code conference and gets led off the stage by some nice guy with a clipboard. Mostly because my dad doesn't know when his own jokes are over or when to stop waiting for people to laugh, or when to pay attention to Clipboard Guy waving at him from the wings.

"It's super safe, Dad," I said. "They wouldn't let kids do it if it wasn't. Consider it my civic duty. That's a good thing, right? You raised a kid who wants to help? Besides, your generation caused climate change, so now here's me and Pete trying to do something about the fires that are your fault."

"I use cloth grocery bags," Dad said with a genuine laugh. "And I recycle."

"While driving your gigantic truck."

"That is the only way to get snow machines where they need to go," he said. "Which you don't complain about at all."

"You're a good person, Dad." I patted him on the shoulder. "Now sign."

But now I don't even want to go to Fire Camp. I just can't imagine it right now. I don't have the energy to scale a climbing wall in a forty-pound suit or run backward dragging a two-hundred-pound dummy with me. I don't want to do trust exercises like doing a ropes course blindfolded, with Pete—or worse, some stranger—talking me through it from the ground. I don't want to eat in a loud mess hall with twenty other teenagers I don't know. I don't want to put in the effort to get to know them, even though they're probably as close to a posse as I'll ever get. After all, what kind of weirdo wants to run into the fire when everyone else is packing up their cars with their dogs and their clothes and driving in the other direction? I don't want to sit in a classroom and pretend that I can focus on all the statistics when I just want to remember how Gigi put her fingers to her ear whenever she was being serious, and how she put that same hand to her collarbone if she was lying to you. Who cares how many hectares burned last year when Gigi isn't on this planet anymore? I want to make a mental inventory of all the movies we ever watched together and then rewatch them, not learn about forest floor management, emergency evacuations, ropes. I don't care how it will look on my college application, which is perhaps the only reason my dad signed that permission letter. There won't be any college anytime soon.

I blew that out of the water.

I just want to stay home.

I don't want to go anywhere.

The Day After I Did Not Get My Cast Cut Off

I am stoned. Over the last two weeks, I've eaten all the edibles—gummy bears, cookies, two lollipops. I was saving the last bottle of Gigi's THC tincture for Fire Camp, although now that I'm not going, I might crack into it when her weed runs out. For now, I am lying on her bed, crosswise, sucking on the vaporizer she bought when she was first diagnosed with cancer. It's like something a Hollywood starlet with pin curls would smoke while reclined on a chaise lounge. I haven't lain in her bed properly since the night she died, because sometimes I think I might never get up. So I lie like this, or sometimes on the floor, or I sit in her pastel pink recliner in front of her TV.

Dust motes dance lazily in the light between the curtains, weaving in and out of the curls of steam from the vaporizer. I can hear the toilet running, which used to drive Gigi mad. Dad fixed it three times, but not since she died. He says it's pretty sad when a running toilet makes you think of someone you loved.

The neighbor is mowing his lawn, which I swear he does twice a day. Or maybe it's because even when he's not mowing, I hear it. Like when you're vacuuming and you hear your phone ringing, even if it's not.

Farther down the block, a bunch of kids are running through a sprinkler, screeching and laughing. Gigi loved the sound of kids playing, even during a super-quiet part in a movie. She never turned it up, and so sometimes we watched entire nighttime spy missions with the soundtrack of red rover or tag.

Dad's sprinkler is spitting and arcing one way over his prize peas, then the other, over his cucumbers. Back and forth.

If I am stoned, these things should not matter. If I am stoned, then why am I still worrying about how to tell Pete that I'm not going to Fire Camp? Why am I still rehearsing the conversation that I don't want to have? Why can't I just be still, with nothing in my head but a low, pleasant buzz?

Pete, you're going to hate me, but . . .

Pete, I don't know how to tell you this . . .

Pete, would you forgive me if I ruin everything?

For once in my life, I kind of just want Pete to leave me alone. Not because I don't want to be with him, but because I don't want him to be with me when I'm like this.

The incredibly tedious *Chariots of Fire* is just about to start on the Movie Classics Channel for the second time today. Gigi loved this movie. She knew long sections of the dialogue by heart and could play that song on the piano. It says something when a song sounds the same even if the piano hasn't been tuned in years. The piano was my mom's thing.

But I'm not changing the channel. In honor of Gigi, her TV will only ever play the Movie Classics Channel, as it has done ever since she moved in.

I suck on the vaporizer and reach for my pen and my notebook. These things that I hear and see are poetic. The dust motes belong in a poem. Gigi was always saying that as she jotted things down in her notebook. "This belongs in a poem, absolutely. It needs a home in a poem." And then a year later, she'd show me the poem with the angled sunlight or the small child's shoes or the broken fence in it. But when I try to describe something that should have a home in a poem, even my writing looks scratchy and weak on the paper. *Glimmer wisps. Slanted glow.* Gigi would say, *Your muse is out running errands. She'll be back when she's found the right eye shadow.*

Said the woman who only ever wore Max Factor.

Here it comes. The beach-running opening. All those fit, young, exclusively white men in their white shorts and white shirts and bare feet, and the guy with the goofy grin.

A commercial for laundry detergent.

Car insurance.

Old-age home.

Mute.

A draft catches the drapes and they lift away just a little, exposing more light and all the dust swirling inside it. This is the poem I've been trying to write since before Gigi died. One good poem. To capture these tiny things that have loomed so large since Gigi came home to die.

I open my notebook and thumb through the pages of half starts and crossed-out lines.

> *~~Dust motes like translucent~~*
> *Outside, I hear the noises of normal life, and I wonder*
> *If they've ever felt loss like this, heavy and sour, like*

A piece of paper falls out. *That* piece of paper. The one that I put in recycling and then took out again three times. I don't know why I'm keeping it. It's not going to make me change my mind about anything.

> As per our conversation in May, we regret to inform you that Annie has not achieved a sufficient GPA to move into twelfth grade. Even with summer school, she will need to redo her junior-year coursework in full. If you have any questions, please do not hesitate to call.

The letter from Principal Hazan came before Gigi died, but I didn't tell her about it, and neither did my dad. He read it, then took it to work with him. Later, in the driveway when he got home, he texted me to come outside. I stood on the stoop, arms crossed, ready to get into a fight. Dad stood there in his code enforcement officer uniform that is a size too small, the paper folded in one hand, his lunch box in his other.

"I'm guessing you don't want Gigi to know about this?"

I shook my head.

"Probably because you and I both know the only reason you're not at school is because of her."

I nodded.

"And I said that was okay, right? Because what was I going to do? Physically force you to go?"

I shook my head.

"No. Because I'm not that dad. And you're not that kid. And you have one grandmother, and she is more than that in so many ways, and we want to do right by her, correct?"

I nodded again. This was one of those lectures that if I talked, I'd only make it worse. So I didn't. Nods, gestures, acceptable. Words? Defense? Not the right time.

"So I said that was okay, so long as Pete brought your work to you and you stayed caught up. That's what I said, right?"

I nodded again.

"Speak up anytime, Banana." I could tell by his voice that he wanted to be angrier too. "Tell me what your plan is."

My turn. Only I didn't have anything good to say. "I don't have a plan."

"You had one. To do your schoolwork."

"While Gigi is dying?"

"That was the deal. I'm pretty sure that you don't want me to go in there and tell her about this letter."

"You wouldn't! She'd just feel guilty. On her deathbed!"

"Okay, then. How about your plan?"

"I don't have a plan, Dad."

"I've got one. You do your junior year over."

"I am not going back."

"The hell you're not. You go back. Redo the year. You broke your end of the bargain, so now I get to decide."

"You can't make me go, Dad. You're not that dad. You just said."

He didn't say anything for a moment. Just stared two holes right through me with his disappointment.

"Online, then," he said. "Those are your two choices."

No. I was not going to do that either. No more school, online or in person. Not for now. But I nodded, because all of it could wait while Gigi was busy actively dying.

He approached me and gave me a tight hug. Even with his hands full, he gives the best hugs, as if he's doing it on behalf of my mom too. One parent, twice the love.

The front door opens and closes.

"Annie?"

Pete.

"In here."

I leap off of the bed and throw open the window. The room stinks of apple-scented pot, and sheets that need to be washed because I haven't changed them since Gigi *died on them*, and me, who needs to be washed too. It's been at least four days since I've showered. When he walks into the room, I'm sitting up on the edge of the bed, with the men of *Chariots of Fire* running around a track while even more white people yell from the stands, each and every one of them dressed in beige or cream or brown. One could almost believe that I've been functionally upwardly mobile in the hours before he walked into the room. Pete tosses his *I ♥ Unicorns* trucker hat onto Gigi's bed and holds up a greasy paper bag. Gigi never let him eat with his hat on.

"Falafel and pakora." Then he frowns. "You still have your cast."

"Interesting food combo."

"Got a problem with it?"

"Nope."

"Cast?"

"Car died."

"Car died. Just a few weeks after being fixed from the crash?"

"Correct."

"Died. Huh."

"Yeah." I glance down at the floor for a second and then tell him the truth, because we suck at lying to each other. "Okay, the car is fine. I just couldn't do it." I lift my broken arm. My not-broken-anymore arm. "I don't want to cut through her flowers."

"The only other option is to let your arm atrophy even more, until the cast can just slip off. You might not ever regain full use of it, though. Hold this." He hands me the bag and pulls the bedside table to his knees and starts unloading the take-out boxes.

"Falafel and pakora don't really go together, Pete."

"Fried and fried goes together," he says. "Preet's mom serves fries with her samosas. She knows what she's doing. She'll be here soon. Not her mom. Preet, I mean."

"How was the thing yesterday?" I will myself to ask it. I just don't like bringing Preet up when she's not even here. It's like it drains the time I *do* get with him, but I know I should ask.

"They had actual caviar," he says. "The black stuff you see in movies. Kind of gross watching people eat it. Especially when they licked their lips after and there were tiny, shiny black bits of fishy nasty rolling everywhere."

"Unicorn Pete here." I do my best impression of him. "Reporting live from a decidedly not-vegan buffet."

"They did have these little cards that said if things were vegan, or had nuts, or gluten, or whatever. Even kosher."

"Rich people."

"Love their little printed card labels that look like they were sloppily handwritten."

"And calling the servers by their first name to acknowledge that they see them as *people.*" We've done enough serving gigs at the ecology center to know the type. "Thanks so much for the pakora, Peter. It looks really great, Peter. I mean, really great, Peter. Do you have plans for college, Peter? Tell me you have plans for college. Because we have to get you out of this station, and I don't mean salads."

"Hey, I did that," Pete says. "To Clive, who brought out

a new platter of these amazing smoked tofu and watercress things."

"Clive probably thought you were hitting on him."

"He was cute."

"Did you introduce Clive to your girlfriend? The one the buffet was honoring?"

"She was off filling her plate with five pounds of gourmet vegetarian hors d'oeuvres."

"What did she think of the little black pearls of fishy loveliness?"

"She says if there was ever a reason she's vegetarian, caviar is it."

"Not being Hindu?"

"Besides that. And anyway, her brother eats meat all the time, even if their parents have no idea."

"Scandal!" I head off to the kitchen and come back with a load of stuff left over from Gigi's not-dead-yet party. Paper plates with illustrations of chandeliers on them. Clear forks. "Like something out of *Cinderella,*" Gigi said when we picked them out. I told her that we had enough plates for us, Pete and his dad, Preet, the doctor, and the two home care nurses. She didn't want anybody else, yet she did want to plan a party for two dozen people. Which is why we have a lot left over, including entire trays of sausage rolls in the freezer and two boxes of the red wine only she would drink. My dad likes cheap wine and cheaper beer, but even he won't drink it.

Pete loads a plate with food and hands it to me.

"Want to?" I hold out the vaporizer. "Before we eat?"

"I think this thing is overheating from overuse." He takes it from me and switches it off.

"Want to crack into one of those boxes of wine?"

"Definitely not," Pete says. "I know she always said it was for her migraines, but I think that stuff gives most people migraines."

"We could make sangria."

"No we could not, because that stuff tastes like ass."

"You're lucky that she's not here to kick said ass of yours."

It's only when I get Pete to myself that we can ever have a drink together. When Preet is around, he doesn't drink at all, because she doesn't. Solidarity.

"The cast has to come off," he says through a mouthful of pakora and tamarind sauce. "It's not an option. Your arm will atrophy even more if you don't. We're going to go after lunch."

I don't say anything because I do know that it's ridiculous to want to keep the cast on only because Gigi drew on it. I know it, even if I don't feel it. The doorbell rings.

"Preet," I whisper while Pete bounds out of the room. I tuck my hair behind my ears and wipe the corners of my mouth with one of the flimsy paper take-out napkins and sit a little taller, all in the seconds I have before she'll step into the room, leaving a wake of Good Person floating behind her, unpretentious and shimmering and dappled with tiny pink cherry blossoms—like the ones decorating her phone cover, her backpack, her clothes, and pretty much everything else she owns, including her climbing helmet, which I bought when I saw it at REI and then gave to Pete to give to her for Christmas.

I hear them talking quietly in the hall, but I can't make out what they're saying. I feel like an invalid, like my caregivers are conferring with each other while I wait in the sickroom with the ruffled periwinkle curtains and the stained and flattened powder-blue shag carpet—the same color as Gigi's eye shadow, which was entirely on purpose—a line of her medicine bottles at attention on the shelf beside the bed. I still haven't thrown them out, which somehow seems connected to not cutting off my cast.

Gigi's clothes—still smelling of Chantilly—hang in the closet exactly how she had them, arranged by color and, within that, by length, tops at one end, dresses at the other. Dad came in with boxes the other day, but then he turned around without saying a word when he saw my face.

Preet comes into the room first, the scent of her just behind her. Sweet, lemony, and a bit of almond, maybe. I can't remember what her perfume is, but it's expensive. The two scents do not mix well. Pete wanted to buy her some perfume for her birthday, so we drove over an hour to the big mall in Bellingham. He had fifty dollars in his wallet, and it was nearly double that. I loaned him the rest, but I never got it back. That's okay, though, that's how we roll. It always works out in the end. But I do kind of want to tell her that half of that perfume she's wearing is from *me.* Dollars made from walking dogs after school. Which is not perfumy at all. Or not in a nice way, anyway.

"Hi, Annie." Preet kicks off her sandals and sits cross-legged on the floor, which looks exceptionally dirty around her. Pete stands there for a moment, and I know what he's thinking. Come sit on the bed with me? Or sit on the floor with Preet? He stands by the door, in between us.

Preet picks up a piece of pakora with her slender brown fingers, her nails short and fingertips stubbed from rock climbing, which she never did before a few months ago, since Pete gave her the cherry blossom helmet. Pete's nails are the same, and mine usually are too. Not lately, though. Now they're just bitten raw, like when Pete and I were little.

"Did you get any chutney, Peter?" Her British accent makes everything sound covered in cherry blossoms, even his full name, which no one else calls him, not even his dad. It's a storybook accent, from a book in which all the lovely ladies and tidy children have a tea party laid out on a blanket in the meadow just below the castle. Parasols. There would be parasols. And a perambulator made out of white rattan. Because "perambulator" sounds so much more posh than "stroller." But there would be a Slip 'N Slide on a grassy knoll, and an archery target range, because even as fancy as she sounds, she is equal parts not. And the cherry blossoms. Must not forget those, falling like sweet pink snow all around.

"I totally forgot," Pete says.

I glance up at him. Forgot about the perambulator?

"You probably have three kinds of chutney," he replies to my blank look. "All homemade by your dad."

"Two. Fridge. Bottom shelf." My words come out thick and soft in the middle. Half-baked.

"I'll go see, shall I?" Preet collects a stack of dirty dishes and takes them with her.

"You, me, your stanky old cast." Pete sits beside me on the bed and tosses his trucker hat toward the door, where it catches on the knob. He's gotten very good at hooking it in one try ever since Gigi stopped eating in front of the TV in the living room and moved in here permanently for the last month of her life and we started eating in here with her, and then kept eating in here even when she stopped eating. VSED. Voluntary Stopping of Eating and Drinking. Which is how she chose to hasten her death.

He knocks on my cast. "Earth to Annie."

"Yeah?"

"Repeat. I'm taking you to get it off. Right after lunch."

Preet comes back with a jar of mango chutney.

"Perfect," she says. At first I think she's talking about the chutney, but then she says, "You can't very well go to Fire Camp with that cast still on, can you? There will be a lot of water, I imagine. And a *lot* of dirt."

I have an image of Fire Camp that keeps coming to me every time I think of me and Pete actually getting there, and it makes no sense. It was a dream at first, of walking up a long dirt road with the bunkhouses off in the distance, fire burning on both sides of us. Trees ablaze and crackling and scorched limbs falling. A searing, shapeless heat suffocating us. I know that I'm just conflating the two words, but I wish it were a campfire, which would also make sense if a brain is going to play tricks on you.

I squeeze my eyes shut and picture that campfire instead. Between the bunkhouses, just above the little mountain lake the camp edges up to. When I open my eyes, Pete and Preet are standing in the doorway.

"I have to go, Annie." She's stuffing a pakora into the pita bread with the falafel in it. "I've got to write a lot more thank-you notes before my flight leaves, or my grannie will meet me at the airport in India and slap my wrist before she even kisses my cheeks."

"For the scholarship?"

"For the money we raised for the school."

I smile and nod. Smile and nod. Even though I helped with the book sale and the car wash and the charity auction and the Bollywood danceathon, I cannot talk about the girls' school Preet's family supports in Chennai, where most of her family still lives. If I talk about it out loud, I might veer way off into snark. That would be okay if it were in reaction to her being holier-than-thou, I-am-so-*nice* fake. But she's actually nice in a *nice* way, in a way that would make me look doubly shallow and desperate if I brought out even an ounce of snark.

I love Pete, and he says that he loves her, so I do my best—my very, very, very best—to let Preet in.

But providing an education for underprivileged girls that includes feminist theory, self-defense training, and basic home repair is simply too much. It is a cartoon, just about. It's not, only because if you met her doctor parents, you'd understand that they're the type of people who want every girl, not just theirs, to have real opportunity.

And so I don't say anything.

I just look at the two of them and marvel yet again at how they are so painfully beautiful, both individually (though I wish I could take away points from Preet for being overly perfect) and especially when they are in close proximity. Then they are a supernova.

Right now they look like storybook parents. Standing in the doorway together, pleased with themselves for the talk about Something Hard they just had with their difficult kid, who they love unconditionally and will not give up on, no matter what. This is how it goes with the three of us. I'm the one screwing up. I'm the one that doesn't quite fit the dynamic, and I want to know how the hell this happened, when it had just been Annie and Pete since we were seven years old, and we never even had to worry about an outsider until Preet came along, because no one wanted to be our third. We were losers—the lanky, weird, unicorn-obsessed Pete, who could survive by himself in the forest if he had a fishing hook and some line, and me, who came to school with only cod liver oil capsules and dried kelp in my lunch, wearing clothes that my mom had dyed purple in the washing machine on purpose (she said it was the strongest color in my aura), or who didn't come at all because my mom could not get out of bed and my dad was still living in Bellingham and Gigi was still renting movies to college kids in Corvallis in her shop that boasted no fewer than a dozen chandeliers of all sorts and sizes. Movies Make It Better, Baby had walls lined with actual movies that they could pick up, bring to her at the front, pay money for, and bring back in a few days. She said it wasn't my fault, that she had to sell the shop anyway because of the internet, but the truth was that the college kids loved her and her chaise lounge at the back, where she draped herself and watched *The Maltese Falcon* and the original *Hairspray* with equal enthusiasm between customers.

She and my dad were in talks, though, about when they'd have to do something about Movies Make It Better, Baby. She saw it coming first. She had that place closed up within half an hour of getting the call from me telling her that I hadn't seen my mom in three days but that was okay, I'd used my Christmas money at the grocery store and was using only the toaster oven for my Pop-Tarts and not the real oven.

I'm sure it took her the usual five hours to drive to me, but it seemed like she suddenly showed up at the front door, like a fairy-tale nanny, shoulders pulled back, a carpetbag over her arm, and a stern look on her face. That stern look was only for my mother's disappearance, and the instant she laid eyes on me, she smiled and reached out and folded me into her layers of silk and lace and so much drapey polyester that I had to pull away to get a good breath.

"Let's get on with things, shall we?" Fancy words with a dumpy rural accent. Music to my ears. "I've been in touch with your father, and he says, and I quote, 'I love you, Banana. I will phone you later. In the meantime, be a dear and help your Gigi find all the gold there is in the house and dump it discreetly into her hideous carpetbag.' "

"He didn't say that."

"This carpetbag, I should tell you, was a prop for the *Mary Poppins* production at the Majestic that I wrote and starred in."

"Wrote and starred in," I chimed in.

"It was a very important moment in my career," Gigi said. She peeled off her gloves and swung off her cape and settled into the living room in front of the TV. "Now, what's on?"

She moved in permanently after that, because my dad couldn't leave his job in Bellingham and no one wanted to take me away from Pete or our school. Gigi didn't want to live in Bellingham either, even though my dad told her that she could probably open up a Movies Make It Better, Baby and make a killing.

"I've lost interest," Gigi said. "We shall stay in Sedro, because where else would your mother go when she decides to come home?"

"When will that be, Gigi?"

"You cannot guess," Gigi said. "You simply have to pray that she is safe, and make space for her here so when she does come home, it's not like she's trying to pull up a chair that doesn't exist to a supper table that doesn't exist."

"We eat in front of the TV."

"Room on the couch, then."

"I can sit on the floor."

"Darling, we always leave a space. For her. Not to be used by anyone else in the meantime. Not one that relegates anyone else to the floor. Your mommy is what you call *eccentric,* and accommodations must be made." She spun to look at my father, stuck a pointer finger in his direction. "Don't say a word."

"Will I get eccentric?"

"No!" Dad bellowed the word. "You won't. You've got half of me, thank Christ."

"See, it doesn't sound like you're actually thanking Christ," Gigi said. She kissed the top of my head. "You come by it naturally, darling. Differently, but it's there." A pat on my head as she drifted by in her silk kimono and with her cigarette sticking out of the long black holder. "Try not to let it get the best of you as you get older. An odd child is one thing, but an odd adult, well. That's altogether different. When your mother was a little girl, she was as strange as the day is long. Piano, piano, piano for days and days and weeks and weeks, breakfast, lunch, and dinner. Then nothing but tears and doomsday and holy ghosts for a month after that."

◇ ◇ ◇

Pete knows what to look for, in my brain. The times I'm not myself, or I'm too much myself. Without him, I would worry that I was falling off of normal into something unrecognizable. He and I are two equal parts. It takes only two halves to make a whole. Not two halves and another bit. Preet has altered the original equation. Adapted the creatures we were into creatures that we are *now,* even if I want things to go back to how it was before. Before Preet. Before Gigi died. Before the crash.

Maybe even all the way back to our moms, because if I'm going to rewrite history, I might as well change the hardest parts first. Because, believe it or not, losing Gigi wasn't even the hardest part.

Packing like a Pro

JUNE 18

The nurse asks me privately if it's okay with me if my boyfriend comes in, or if I'd rather he wait outside. Pete's standing behind me, my bag over his shoulder, grinning. It never occurred to me that he wouldn't come in, but now that it's an option, it appeals for some strange reason.

"She says just me," I say to him with a shrug.

The nurse shrugs too as she leads me into the room. She doesn't want to wreck Gigi's garden either, so she and I find a route through the flowers that is not the straight line like on the casts before me, quick and dusty and chucked in the garbage after. She knows a piece of art when she sees it.

"You did all this yourself?"

"My grandma."

"She's quite the artist," she says. "I'd like a purse in this design."

"Right? I want sheets, shoes, a bathing suit."

"A journal." She starts the saw. "Underwear." She begins to slice. "You tell her our ideas. I expect a cut." She winks, her smile so genuine and easy that I am not going to wreck it.

"I will," I say. "She's waiting in the car."

"What kind of car does she drive?"

"A 1972 Aston Martin."

"Of course she does."

It is done in less than a minute. She gently slides the cast over my hand now that it has the extra give.

"Go glue that up," she says. "And say hi to your grannie for me."

"I call her Gigi."

"Which is perfect." She smiles. "Take care, both of you."

The cast smells like sweat and dead skin, but I don't care. I put it on the sill in my room. Before he goes to meet Preet at her house, Pete gives me a squishy ball and a set of those hand clamp exercisers.

"To get you back up to strength," he says. He kisses me on the forehead and then wrinkles his nose. "Either you or the cast reeks."

"Either you or your asshole is an asshole." I throw the ball at him as he retreats.

For the last two nights, I've slept in my room, which is the first time since we brought Gigi home from the "Your Life,

Your Death, Your Choice" doctor visit. The sheets are crisp and clean, but a bit musty too. Gigi would want me in here now. *Now when the denouement comes, Annie. Never ignore the denouement.*

I'm not certain, but I think this is it. The strands of the story are brought together. Everything is resolved.

When I say "the last two nights," I actually mean "for most of the last two nights," which is still an accomplishment. On the first night back in my room, I made it to midnight and then spent the rest of the night curled up in Gigi's bed watching a Hitchcock marathon. The second night, I made it to just before dawn, and then I watched *Animal House* three times back to back.

But I'm trying.

Pete calls when the *Animal House* marathon rolls into a Patrick Swayze one, starting with *The Outsiders,* which might be in my top ten Brat Pack movies.

"Can't talk," I say. "Ponyboy just opened the composition book."

"Listen, what's something of mine that you really want to take to Fire Camp?"

Ten days to Fire Camp and I haven't told Pete that I'm not going.

"I love your unicorn flip-flops so much," I say. "Look, he's getting chased by the jerks in the car. I should go. He might need my help."

"Tell me you want my unicorn flip-flops so bad."

"I want them so bad," I say. "So, so bad."

"I *knew* it! You like them because they're translucent and sparkly."

"You're on the porch, right?"

"You want them," Pete says. He lowers his voice and makes it way too seductive, all things considered. "Say it again. Say you want them nice and deep in your backpack."

Not even a minute later, he's at my bedroom door in overalls rolled up a few times, a sleeveless shirt, and bare feet, his disgusting flip-flops in hand. He holds them out, like an offering.

How is it that he could be wearing a McDonald's uniform and he would still be the hottest person for five blocks in any direction? He's asking me something.

"What?"

"Are you high?" he says again.

"Actually, no."

"Good. We need to focus."

"Can I have a side of fries?"

"What?"

"Sorry, inside joke."

"Annie, Annie, Annie." He puts his hands on my shoulders. I love it when he does this, because it's usually when I feel like I'm about to float off into la-la land or rage land or hysterical land, and his hands are like reassuringly heavy sandbags, which might not seem like a romantic thing, but actually is. "Inside jokes for *one* don't really make any sense. Because then they're not really *inside* anything, right?"

I reach up to put my hands on his shoulders, and lean forward until our foreheads are touching. There is that lovely, low pulse I feel when we do this. "News flash," I say. "Joke's inside of *me.* Party of one. Boom!" I jump back, arms spread. "Right? That's right."

He rolls his eyes.

My face falls when I remember that I have to tell him that I'm not doing Fire Camp.

"What?" Pete says. "What's wrong?"

I've just realized something. Why *wouldn't* I do Fire Camp? Just because I flunked eleventh grade and my grandma died? Well, okay, two very good reasons not to go, but also, two very good reasons to go. Especially because going will get my dad off my back about my plans for the fall. Which I do not have at all.

"I was just thinking about what a terrible packer you are, and how I've got a lot of work ahead of me if we're going to be ready to drive up there in ten days. Well, actually, ten days is way too much time. Why are you even here, Pete?"

"You know me so well."

"You're an even worse last-minute packer than I am."

"I'm turning over a new leaf?"

"You are not."

For a moment, he lets me guess, or he thinks that's what he's doing.

"Not guessing," I say.

"Really? Maybe just one guess?"

"We got the dates wrong and Fire Camp started yesterday."

"Nope."

"Give."

"My flip-flops."

"Give!" I grab them and march to the front door and chuck them as far as I can. "Now fetch."

"I can live without them," he says.

"And I can live without knowing what you have up your sleeve."

"You can't."

"I can so."

"You, Annie Poltava, absolutely cannot."

"You and Preet are pregnant."

"Not funny."

"I would make a great auntie, though." He stares at me. "I don't know. Just tell me. Or settle down and shut up and watch Ponyboy's life unravel."

"Let me get something from my truck."

I watch the TV for the two minutes it takes him to get his backpack.

"I thought we were doing duffel bags," I say.

He hands me a small cardboard box and then takes another out of his pack and holds on to it, not opening it.

"These are from Preet," he says. "But she says don't open them yet. Actually, on second thought." He takes back my box and puts them both into the pocket under the lid of his pack. We call that our safe, and each of us packs important things in there, like our ID, money. My Altoids tin full of talismans is in mine, with the square of pyrite I found, and the little Idaho star garnet I spotted in the purple sand of the creek in the Nez Perce National Forest when Pete's dad took us there three summers ago.

"I'll take care of them," Pete says as he zips up the pocket and flips the lid over. "Preet has a plan."

I completely forgot that Preet is gone now. To India, until September. Remembering this doesn't make me happy, exactly. Or not quite. It makes me feel a bit untethered. Like if this were a movie, I'd spend until then trying to be the Good Person I want to be, while fighting the urge to mess it up for her by doing something a Bad Person would do, like telling Pete that Preet is the wrong person for him, because I'm his only person.

"Show, don't tell," my mom used to instruct her piano students. "Show us the song. Show us what you think of the song. *Show* your feelings. Don't just play the notes."

Don't just say the words.

But how to show it? That's not what we do. Maybe I should lean in for the second kiss I've been waiting so long for, maybe when we're head to head, looking for minnows at the edge of a marsh with fluffy cattails tall and shedding all around us. Or at night, just after we've turned our headlamps off and put the Uno cards away. If only there were someone to ask. But there's just Pete, which is exactly the problem/not-problem. There he is, standing in front of me, saying words that I'm not hearing.

Focus, Annie.

"So here's some news," he's saying. "We're hiking to Fire Camp."

One good long look at his face and I can tell that he is completely serious.

"I can't just leave, Pete."

"Yes you can," he says. "I checked with your dad. I gave both dads the maps, routes highlighted."

He pulls me up and out of the room before I can formulate a response. He steers me down the hall to the door that leads to the basement. Where half of our camping gear is kept. The other half is at his house. It only works together, though. Like, I have the stove. He has the fuel. That sort of thing.

"What route?"

"That part of the Pacific Northwest Trail that evil Jill said was awesome. She took it all the way to Loomis."

"You're taking trail advice from the idiot who said we couldn't be in the same tent based on the shape of our genitals? From the person whose letter we had to expunge from our files?"

"That's a good word," Pete says. *"Expunnnnnge."*

"And it wasn't easy!"

"The expunging or the applying it in an appropriate context?"

I just stare at him.

He continues. "I listened to her talk about it with the trail maintenance guy. And it's not like it's the Evil Jill Trail. You and I have hiked parts of the Pacific Northwest Trail before. This is just going to be our first thru-hike. My dad looked at the maps, and he agrees that we can do it. It's rough in some parts, but then there's lots of alpine too."

"The flowers won't even be out yet."

"Some will."

"And grizzlies?"

"Doing their own thing, as usual. That's your department."

"Our spray is expired."

"My dad says it's fine for a long, long, long time after."

"Can he get us a new one?"

Pete shakes his head. "We're leaving today."

"Wait." I drop everything. "Now?"

"As soon as we're packed."

"I can't." I look around for something tangible to be my excuse. "What about the dogs?"

Our dog-walking business, which I haven't helped with since Gigi died.

"Preet's little brother is taking it over until we get back."

I keep staring.

"He's saving up for a car."

We both laugh. That would take a thousand dogs.

"But I have to—"

"You don't have to anything." Pete grabs my toiletry bag and starts rooting through it. "Gigi's gone. And you have to get out of this house and remember what you love." He holds it out to me. "Where is your EpiPen?"

"Glove box."

"It needs to be in here."

"You told me it should be in the glove box."

"And now it needs to be in with your toothbrush and stuff."

"I'm not ready to go, Pete."

"You will be, once we're on the trail." He grabs my pack off the shelf, floppy and worn and still smelling of dirt. "Come on. Let's get packing."

"Pete? Seriously?" I peer into the toiletry bag. My toothbrush, the handle cut in half to save weight. A small tube of toothpaste. A couple of spare tampons. Where's my DivaCup? I shouldn't need it, but I like to have it just in case. Bug bite cream. Two hair ties. Not even a comb. I may, in fact, be a Neanderthal when we're in the backcountry. I should at least add dental floss. Some Dr. Bronner's.

"I've got a little thing of Bronner's," Pete says. "And I've already packed all the food. And loaded the water bladders. And yes, I cleaned them first. Would you be inspired and amazed to hear that our dads paid for all the food? And your dad paid for the trail pass too."

"So he's okay with me just going? So soon?"

"He thinks it's just what you need." Pete stuffs my sleeping bag into the compression sack and then wedges it at the bottom of my pack, just where I like it. "He'll be here to say goodbye."

"Maybe I don't want to say goodbye?"

Pete takes my favorite pair of hiking socks out of a pack pocket and throws them at me, then tosses me one of my hiking shoes and then the other. They don't look much different from running shoes, but they act more like hiking boots, without the bulk. Good tread, structured heel, but super flexible too, for jumping from rock to rock, or over streams, or scrambling up hills. Okay. Now I'm getting excited. But I still want a day or two to—

What? Watch a *Police Academy* marathon or *Sophie's Choice,* just to recite the lines to the empty room?

"It's not dead-goodbye, Annie. It's a see-you-in-a-few-weeks kind of goodbye. 'I'm almost an adult, Dad' kind of goodbye. 'Trying not to be a screwup here, Dad' kind of goodbye. 'I'm a capable and smart person who should not waste her summer—or life, for that matter—watching the Movie Classics Channel, Dad' kind of goodbye."

"Enough," I say. "I get it."

Pete says he got everything we need from his house earlier and we don't have to go there on the way out of town, which is a serious olfactory relief, because Pete's basement is like a giant, smelly used-outdoor-gear store. That pong of it all makes my eyes water. You can even smell it upstairs too, if they leave the door open. Musty, fungusy, dirty, but it does have everything you'd need for ice climbing, a bicycle trek in Tasmania, a thru-hike in Bolivia, a kayak trip through class 5 rapids, or BASE jumping in Turkey. Pete's dad has done all of that, and still does all of that, even though his best friend died when he jumped off a cable car in Turkey and was sailing down with his squirrel wings out but then hit the rocks before he hit the water. Everett pulled Luca out, but he was lifeless. Everett said he would never jump again, but then he found a letter that Luca had written to him in case anything happened during one of all their crazy stunts, about their friendship and how they saw life, and how miraculous the planet is and how it's good to be alive today, which Pete and I say to each other all the time. It's from a song by Michael Franti, soul rocker and troubadour. Everett took us to see him play at the Gorge, which was about as magical as it gets, with a pink sunset beyond the stage, and thousands of beautiful people nestled almost shoulder to shoulder in the gap between high bluffs, like a cauldron of sparkling hope with the stars popping into place as night fell.

Pete and I both carry relatively small packs for backcountry hiking, like Pete's dad taught us to, and like Luca taught him. Sometimes we see other hikers on the trails and they've got packs so heavy that they have to put them down on a waist-high log to get them off, and then they have to put them back on the same way.

I hear a whistle from upstairs, and heavy steps.

Then there's my dad, who prefers his hunting trailer to a tent, and a generator's rumble to nature's silence. But he doesn't mind if I want to sleep on the ground or hike off to wherever. He lets me go do exactly that pretty much anytime, anywhere. There's not much he doesn't let me do, and it's not because he's ignorant of the shit Pete and I get up to, but because he's a firm believer that if you try to hold someone back, they'll only use greater force to run away.

Which is what happened with Mom, so Pete and I don't doubt his parenting philosophy—if he even sees it as a "philosophy." Instead, I am ever grateful for his blissfully long leash, and he is ever grateful for my level head.

Pete's level head, that is.

"Down here, Dad." I will admit that even just pulling out the bin with our folding stove packed into my titanium pot is getting me excited. Sporks, collapsible bowls/mugs, leftover packets of hot chocolate from last time. "Did you bring the tent from your house, Pete?"

"Yup. Not the fly, though." Usually, he carries the tent, I carry the poles, and then we switch on the way back. "It's not going to rain. We'll save weight."

My dad comes down the stairs. He has to duck too, but he's a good two inches shorter than Pete now. He's come home to say goodbye with his code enforcement officer uniform still on, big sweat stains under his arms, buttons straining against his beer belly.

"Pretty good surprise Pete had for you, right, kiddo?" He picks up a plastic bag and then drops it right away when he sees that it's my DivaCup. "Sorry about that." His cheeks go red, just like mine, even though he's way less weird about body stuff than a lot of parents. "Just what you need, I think."

"The cup?" I laugh.

"No, smart-ass. This trip, with Pete." He hugs me to him. "You need to *go.* Get *outside.* You like all that. It works for you. It's exactly what the doctor ordered. And what Gigi would've ordered too."

"You're probably right, Dad." I look up at him, his big, bushy beard all messy like the mountain man he mostly is. A softer version of a mountain man. One that cries and says thank you to a deer when he shoots it. "What'll you do, though? Won't you be lonely?"

"I will absolutely be lonely."

"But you don't mind, I know."

"My garden keeps me company." He squeezes me again. "There will be tomatoes and peppers and watermelons when you get back. And so much kale you will be sick of it within three days." Another squeeze, this one so hard he almost lifts me off my feet. "And all the hummingbirds will keep me company too."

The twenty feeders all around the front lawn and backyard started out as one of my mom's projects. Which fizzled just after the summer during which she'd built and bought and scavenged the feeders and cajoled my dad into planting only red and purple and pink plants so the yard would be a "blazing twenty-four-hour diner under their flight path." The feeders sat empty when she was gone, and then when my grandma moved in, she happily took over the hummingbird project, even though she said she would not be taking up her daughter's fleeting interest in chickens.

Dad took over that. Now he'd have the feeders too.

"A pleasant triumvirate, the chickens, the garden, the hummingbirds."

"Dad?"

"Yes, Banana?"

"You have to let go of me if I'm going to finish packing."

"Yes!" He heads for the stairs. "I'll find you some fruit for the trip." Just as I'm about to remind him that fruit takes up too much room, is too messy, and goes off too soon, he shakes a finger at me.

"I know, I know," he says. "For the ride to the trailhead. Plus, carrots. Which do travel well, so don't say you won't take those."

Rope for hanging up our food for the night, out of the reach of bears, water filtration system, first-aid kit—we'll check that before we go—bug spray, sun hat. I pause for a moment and catch my dad before he's at the top of the stairs.

"You'll really be okay? If I go?"

It's not that he hasn't been alone before. He took a job as a code enforcement officer in Bellingham when I was four and didn't come back except to pick me up until I was eight. He and my mom didn't divorce, but they didn't like being in each other's company either. After Gigi moved in, we waited for my mom to come back so things could be as normal as they ever were. A week went by. Then three. When it was obvious that she might not come back at all, my dad managed to talk the code enforcement office here into casual work and came home. We didn't have much money until he started working there permanently, but that didn't matter. He was here, Gigi was here, and my life seemed calm for once, even if I missed my mom and wondered where she was and what she was doing.

Dad loved Gigi, even if she was his mother-in-law. He clearly got on better with her than he ever did with his wife. Gigi, who sat with him and played cribbage every night between movies even though he never won. Gigi, who would watch action blockbusters with him anytime even though she hated the majority of them. They shopped for groceries like an old married couple, peering through their drugstore reading glasses to report how much sodium was in a can of soup (Gigi, who never cooked) or to see if the tiny print on the sticker on the "fresh" figs said they were actually from South Africa (Dad, because he only bought local when he could).

Now Gigi is gone, and she was his best friend.

"I'll be fine, Banana." He blows me a kiss, and one for Pete too. "I have the chickens and the hummingbirds, and there's tomato blight to conquer. Not to mention the aphid situation."

He stops by his pantry and grabs a jar of peaches.

"Don't talk to me about how much it weighs," he says as he tucks it into the top of my pack. "Eat it at the trailhead and leave the jar in the truck. Done up tight, though. Ants."

"Thanks, Dad." I grab his beefy arm as he steps away. "I love you."

"I love you, kiddo." He pulls me into a bear hug that actually is like being hugged by a bear. Big, hairy, smelly, strong, his beardy chin resting on top of my head. We have this thing where neither of us wants to let go first, but this time I do, because he really does hold on forever.

✧ ✧ ✧

Now that I'm all packed, I am positively looking forward to this. Pete is right. This is exactly what I need to get me out of my head, out of Gigi's room, and off the Scale of Stupid for a while. Or two out of three, maybe, because our tent is about the size of our couch, and if you put two people on a couch, lying down—facing each other or spooning, it doesn't matter—the degree of closeness can significantly up the Scale of Stupid, especially if one of them wants to kiss the other.

Caramels

You can get onto the Pacific Northwest Trail not far from where we live. It's pretty new, still rough, and unmarked in places. It's over twelve hundred miles if you thru-hike from Glacier National Park all the way to the Olympic Peninsula. We've been on parts of it, and both of us volunteered to do trail maintenance last summer near Ross Lake. There was an illegal rave a couple of miles south of our base camp, so Pete and I decided to sneak out and go to it, even though the whole area was on fire watch and our group leaders were waiting to hear if we would have to evacuate because of a wildfire burning across the river from where the rave was.

We walked down the dirt road, with a full moon above so bright and big that we should've been able to see, except the smoke socked everything in, and we had to use our headlamps. It was so thick that by the time we heard the thumping bass half a mile away, we were both surprised that the rave hadn't already been evacuated.

"We should turn back," Pete said.

"No way." I grabbed his arm and we ran the rest of the way. "I am not going to be this close to a real rave and not go."

We walked right in, suddenly finding ourselves in a sea of glow sticks and tiny lights of every color and degree of twinkle and blink wrapped around arms and torsos, feathered angel wings dotted with twinkling lights in blues and greens, and everyone was dancing to the music the DJ spun on a folding table just above the river.

And on the other side of the river? Not even two hundred feet from the bank?

The wildfire. It wasn't supposed to jump the river. Two hours ago, that fire couldn't have. I hadn't noticed the wind change, but here it was, and once a fire is after you, you cannot run fast enough. Sometimes you cannot even drive fast enough. And it's the unpredictable behavior of a fire like that that makes people abandon their cars in a slow-moving evacuation and start running. A fire can change so fast that it devours entire towns, with people trapped in their homes.

Trees like flaming matches, a writhing carpet of flames covering the forest floor.

"Holy shit," I said.

Then we did the thing you're never supposed to do in a packed theater.

"Fire! Fire!" Pete yelled. "Everybody has to get going now!"

And while it wasn't a movie theater, it was packed, and there were only a few ways out besides impossible bushwhacking. People started screaming and running, grabbing each other's hands and heading away from the river to where the cars were parked. The music kept thumping, and when I glanced up to the stage, the DJ looked oblivious, with his headphones on and the light show still strobing and pulsing behind him.

"We have to go tell him," Pete said.

"Look around you, Pete!" Everyone else on the stage was pulling cables and trying to collect the sound equipment. "He wants to keep going. He'll get out. He's doing the *Titanic*. We have to go!"

I grabbed his hand and we ran. Back up the dirt road, our lungs hurting as we sucked in the smoke. We half expected to be flagged down by the trucks as they evacuated the trail maintenance crew, but we made it all the way back to camp, where we stood, panting, for just a second before we made a beeline for the outdoor kitchen and the tap. I drank so much water that I got a stomachache and almost threw up, but I felt amazing. *Amazing* amazing. The adrenaline ran hot through my veins, and even though most of me wanted to go back, the sane part knew that we had to get some sleep.

Pete and I ran back to the wall tents. Boys in one, girls in the other, no matter how hard we argued to be in the same one. "We're best friends! We've been sleeping in the same tent since we were seven and my grandmother built us a tent out of sheets hung over the clothesline." But they would have none of it. Boys in the boys' tent. Girls in the girls' tent. No exceptions. We kept pushing. "What if we were gay? That's the same as having a boy in the girls' tent and a girl in the boys' tent, right? Because you think we'd have sex? How does that even make any sense?"

"Boys in the boys' tent," Hassam, the boys' leader, said. "No exceptions."

"Girls in the girls' tent," Jill, the girls' leader, said. "No exceptions."

Said the two college kids who we saw leaving those tents and making out on the dirty couches at the back of the camp kitchen.

"We have to tell everyone," I said.

"Right now," said Pete.

"I just need two seconds to gather myself and pretend that what happened didn't. My heart is beating so fast." I pulled his hand to my chest. "Feel it?"

"Me too." He pulled my hand to his chest.

Right then the two tent leaders and the other leaders—trails, tools, kitchen, and logistics—appeared from the far end of the camp, flashlights bobbing like giant fireflies.

"Campers!" Jill shouted.

We dropped hands and leaped apart, even though it would never have occurred to Unicorn Pete that holding hands meant anything more than just plain holding hands.

The logistics leader lifted an air horn and sounded three blasts, adding insult to injury to my ears, which were still ringing from the rave.

Three blasts equals evacuation. So they already knew.

"You two, stop!" Hassam shouted when Pete and I headed for the tents for our packs, already ready to go, which was the way they had us keep them, for exactly this reason.

"I'm going to take three seconds out of this evacuation to tell you this." Jill shone her headlamp in our faces. "You are not welcome back next year. Inappropriate behavior."

"For seeing the fire first?"

"You can't see it from here," she said.

"No, seriously, because we were holding hands?" I shouted, which surprised Jill and me both, considering the incredulous look she gave me. "Seriously? I've known him since I was seven! Do you even *have* a friend like that?"

Without looking away from me, she grabbed the air horn and blasted it three times, exactly in the space between me and Pete.

"Consider it a foot for each blast," she said. "As in, if I see you closer than that, there will be real trouble. Now get your packs and meet at the trucks! Go!"

Pete and I got into the backseat of the truck that the trails leader was driving. He'd seen us get in trouble, but when he finally noticed us back there, shoulder to shoulder, wedged beside the biggest kid in the camp, he just slammed on the brakes for a second, before shaking his head and gunning it to catch up with the convoy.

When we passed the rave, the clearing was empty except for all the trash people had left behind. The parking lot was chaos, with people trying to get out. Cars and trucks and beat-up old vans kicked dirt up, not that you could tell the difference between that and the smoke. And even though people were packing in as many carless strangers as possible, there was still a large group waiting for a ride. It was surreal, seeing all those glowing necklaces and people entwined in fairy lights, like so many elfin evacuees, stranded in the forest.

The muster point was the ranger station, where we waited for Pete's dad to come get us. The smoke wasn't so bad down there, but our clothes and packs stank of it. We sat on the lawn out front, watching everyone bustling around, even if we weren't sure what all the excitement was about, considering there was no wildfire threat down here. Jill hurried back and forth, from the admin building to the sheds at the back, ignoring us mostly, except to throw us the odd increasingly dirty look.

"What can she do?" I could tell by Pete's voice that he was actually asking that, rather than implying that there wasn't anything she could do. "Right?"

What she did do was talk to Pete's dad when he showed up an hour later. She tried to talk to him privately, but Everett wouldn't have that.

"You can say whatever you want in front of them," he said. "Seeing as they're who you're going to talk about, right?"

"I don't care about how long they've been friends," Jill said. "I don't care that they say that they're *just* friends. I don't care if they are gay or straight or bi or ace or queer, in whatever sense of those words, nor do I care if they have sleepovers seven nights a week at both their homes, at the same time." Apparently, she'd been practicing this speech when she was hurrying back and forth, considering how it rolled off her tongue so smoothly now. "The rule here is boys in one tent. Girls in the other. And even though both Pete and Annie are exceptionally hard workers on the trail, the truth is that they might as well have passports to a country with a population of two, and their own language and currency to go along with it, when it comes to being team players."

"Gotcha," Everett said.

"Furthermore, they are not welcome back next summer."

"Gotcha."

"We weren't coming back anyway," I said, like a brat.

"Fire Camp," Pete said, like someone who had just remembered that we needed letters of recommendation from the trail project to get into Fire Camp.

"I'll be in touch with them," Jill said. "I'll make sure they know all about you."

"Gotcha." Everett glanced at me, then Pete. "No point backtracking now. No groveling allowed. That would just poke the bear some more, and you've done enough of that."

"And great." Jill threw up her hands. "You're not taking this seriously either."

"Nope." Everett shrugged. "What, penises in one tent, vaginas in the other?"

"That's not what I said."

"How do you know what's in anyone's pants? And how do you know who wants into anyone else's pants?"

Everett paused, and Jill glared at him.

"Safe drive home," she said, then turned on her heel and walked as fast as she could without running to the admin building.

Everett put an arm over each of our shoulders.

"We don't need a talk, do we?"

"No," Pete said.

"Definitely *no.*" I pressed my hands together under my chin, as if to pray.

The Talk.

Everett and my dad had sat us down *all together* when we were fourteen, because Gigi had said that she was going to do it if they didn't. With cheeks as red as his prized tomatoes, my dad told us not to be stupid, which was fair enough. Advice received. But then Everett told Pete not to, more specifically, put his penis into my vagina. At which point Pete and I slid into a heap on the dirty carpet and howled with horror for the rest of the day. Only, it was less than a minute, because then Everett said that if we did have penis-in-vagina sex, we should use a condom. A condom! My dad leaned forward, head in his hands. Everett offered him a glass of water. Gigi was there with one before Everett could stand up, which meant she had been listening to the whole conversation.

That entire exchange was awkward and horrible for everyone but Gigi, who had a big grin on her face that said she could've done a much better job but this was entertaining as hell.

Penis-in-vagina sex with each other had never occurred to us. Or at least not to me. Until that very moment.

Before we drove home, we climbed up the little hill behind the building, under the power lines, and ate the PB&J sandwiches Everett had taken the time to make before coming to get us. A thermos of cold milk, and apple slices sprinkled with cinnamon too. Pretty much the same meal he'd been making for us since Pete's mom died.

"You two are old enough to make your own choices about your bodies and each other," Everett said. "That's what matters. The dads agree." The moon glowed so bright now that there was hardly any smoke, and we could see to pick the wild strawberries growing all around. I remember that smell most of all. Warm strawberries and smoke and the thought of what it would be like to do the thing that everyone thought we were doing already.

We've just passed May Creek, where the rave was, but instead of heading straight north, Pete takes a cut to the right. He hands me a page protector with five or six sheets of paper. Topographical maps.

"I've got the waypoints in the GPS too."

"Where are we parking?"

Pete shrugs. "We'll find somewhere."

"Where are we going in?" I say. "Why didn't we just park at the trailhead?"

"We're going to go parallel, south of it."

"Why?"

"Less people. And a hot spring that my dad told me about that is epically secret." Pete pulls over and puts the truck into park. "Pee break."

He gets out and goes to the back of the truck, but before he's done, he's waving for me to come. With one hand, obviously. By the time I get out there, he's done and is shushing me with both hands.

"Snakes," he whispers, pointing. Just ahead of us, nestled in a group of boulders on the other side of the road in a wide patch of sun, is a knot of snakes. Just garters, but big ones.

"How many do you think there are?" I ask.

"Maybe five? Six?"

We creep forward. I pull my phone out of my pocket and start a video.

"What do you call a snake that works at a construction site?" Pete asks.

I turn the camera on him.

"I don't know, Unicorn. What do you call a snake that works at a construction site?"

He grins. "A boa *constructor.*"

I laugh, and then I swing the camera back to the snakes because I hear a rustle. They're untangling, and there are eight of them. Skinny, about two feet long each, shiny green-black, slithering into the bush. When the last one has disappeared, I turn the camera back to Pete.

"What's a snake's favorite subject?"

"Hisssssstory," Pete says. Then he hooks his arm across my shoulders and steers me back to the truck, which is already so dusty that it looks like we've been driving for days on this logging road in the middle of absolutely nowhere.

"Did you tell your dad that you changed the route?"

"And yours."

"Did you bring new topo maps too?"

"I didn't have time to print them. But I have them on my phone," Pete says. "Now, I hope you're going to give me my badge for safety and preparedness, because I am all over the safe and prepared on this one. The US Safety and Preparedness badge shall be mine!"

This is a joke we have, the Unicorn Scouts Safety and Preparedness badge. We're not particularly safe or prepared, but we always get away with it. If we worried too much about being safe or prepared, we'd never leave the house. And we would not be here, on a rough road, bouncing along with nearly no shocks—he should've replaced them last fall—fishtailing, correcting. Fishtailing, correcting. Pete does take care of his truck. He's just saving up for new shocks. He calls his truck the Unicorn, but it is not sparkly or graceful. It does have a plastic shimmering horn screwed into the hood at just the right place, though. And it is, perhaps, magic. Because it has never broken down on us. Lift package, exhaust out the top so we can go through puddles the size of small ponds, ham radio and its wobbly antenna like a giant insect that's had the other one broken off, and a decal of a unicorn with its mane blowing in the wind that takes up most of the hood. And about a million other unicorn stickers, many with rainbows, which is maybe why someone once spray-painted *faggot* on the side, and another time scratched *gay* above one of the tires. He's never taken off either.

"How far up this road?" I yell over the music.

"Maybe ten miles?"

"My ass is already numb." I get up onto my knees to check on our packs in the back.

"I tied them in," Pete says. "Don't worry."

They're fine. So dirty now that I wouldn't be able to pick them out of a police lineup, but still sitting side by side, cinched to the strap that runs across, the one that the previous owner used to hook his dog onto.

The truck slides toward the edge on my side. For a moment, I can see straight down, the fallen trees, boulders, and a narrow, rushing river at the very bottom.

"Safety and preparedness!" I shriek, but I'm laughing too as we climb up, up, up. Pete gears down when it gets super steep. I change the music to one of our playlists: Get Your Ass Outside.

It's not mellow, like it might sound. It's DJ Ninja, drum and bass. He played at that rave in the forest, which I didn't know until we got home and I looked it up. And then I had no idea he was so famous until Preet freaked out when I asked if she knew who he was.

We crest the hill and the road levels out. Suddenly we're in rangeland, miles and miles of grassy hills, cattle guards, and open-range warnings.

Pete speeds along this part. Fifty miles an hour, his back end slipping on each corner. We come around a sharp one, and he gears down suddenly and then slams on the brakes to avoid hitting a giant tea party of cows gathered in the middle of the road. They're chewing their cud, their tagged ears flapping at flies, and they're staring at us with big, wet eyes and slimy noses.

We sit there, knowing how this goes.

You wait.

Honking your horn does nothing.

Getting out sometimes makes them skittish enough to move, but they once got too skittish and I had to jump into the back of the truck to avoid being trampled. So we wait.

"Uno?"

"Sure."

There's a deck in the glove box, and a joint too, I discover. I pull out both. I hand him the joint while I start shuffling the cards. He immediately chucks it out the window.

"Pete! What the hell?"

"This is a clean and sober trip," Pete says. "*Clean* clean. Both of us. For the whole trip. No exceptions."

"How about after?"

"Negotiable. Or maybe I should say, it depends. On how Gigi you're going to be."

"I do not have to Gigi," I say.

"'Gigi' is not a verb," he says.

"It can be. And you know it."

"Well, then." He smirks. "I can Annie."

"Which is mostly inspired by Gigi."

So maybe I won't tell him about the last bottle of Gigi's THC tincture. I'll wait until Fire Camp, when Pete isn't so obsessed with his Make Annie Better project. I also have seven mini bottles of vodka from Gigi's stash, which I am definitely not telling him about. Gigi bought those by the box, preferring stashability to economy. She especially liked having half a dozen in her purse at any time. She said they were to give to the homeless guys who lived in the woods behind the Thrifty Mart, which was partially true. But that actually meant two for some guy, four for her. Daily.

Pete will want some of the vodka by the time we get to Fire Camp. We'll mix it with lemonade. Ah, who am I kidding? I'll share the tincture with him too. I love him, and besides, if I get to have it all, I'll probably be sent home before the first week is over. Mind you, it'd be gone by then too.

"See any caramels in there? Probably melted by now." He leans across me to get at the glove box and ends up lying in my lap. I feel that flush I don't want to feel. The one that is so confusing to me, because I thought I sorted through those intrusive feelings last year, when we did kiss. And now there is Preet to think about, because no way am I going to be *that girl.* Those girls are an insult to all the other girls. It would be very, very helpful, universe, if you could show me the way on this one, because right now I just want to lean down, knock his unicorn hat off, take his face in my hands, and kiss him full on the lips.

"Ta-da." He sits up and proudly displays a handful of caramels. He grabs his seven cards.

We play three games. He wins all of them. He wins at mostly everything. But I don't mind.

Some of the cows wander off.

Most don't.

And while we wait, I spend way too much time thinking about that one kiss that should've changed everything.

Dear Heart

The sun is starting to set when the cows move enough to clear a path. Not much farther and we turn off the logging road and onto a rough track with just one set of ruts. If anyone wants to pass, one of us will have to reverse to a more open spot, or climb up onto the low berm that runs alongside the road. Not that you'd necessarily call it that.

"Where the hell are we?"

"Pasayten Wilderness, south of Devil's Ridge."

"I don't know what that means."

"South of the Pacific Northwest Trail. Map seventy-three."

I pull the papers out of the page protector and find the one.

"But these are for the PNT," I say. "We're not on the PNT."

"No, we're just below it," Pete says as he slows to a stop. "The red line is the PNT. We're going to do pretty much the same thing, except a few miles south. These are the best topo maps, and they were free. It'll be close enough. Guaranteed."

"This isn't the route the dads approved, is it?"

"Most of the time, we'll be so close that we can just shout if we want someone to hear us."

"Why this way?" I say. "Why not the PNT?"

He shrugs.

"I know that shrug."

"Then you know the answer."

"Adventure."

"Uncharted territory!" Pete shouts. "By us, anyway."

He speeds up again while I follow the red line, taking note of the elevations. The jar of peaches rolls onto the floor. I put it back on the bench so it doesn't roll under the gas pedal or, worse, the brake. There is a lot of elevation on this path. A serious amount of going up, then down, then repeat.

It's dark enough now that he flips on the row of lights above the cab, on high, illuminating the forest on either side and making it look like something out of a horror movie. And there it is, suddenly bounding out of the bush and onto the road and then turning—

"Deer!" I grip the door handle as Pete cranks the wheel to miss it, and we start to spin out, only the track isn't big enough to go in a complete circle. Pete overcorrects the other way, and for a moment, my heart starts slowing down. It's all good. But then another deer bounces almost cheerfully out from the forest, and this time we ram right into it. The jar of peaches sails through the air and smashes against the windshield, syrup and bits of broken jar and perfect, slippery peach halves sliming up cracked glass. I can feel the impact in my bones. A horrible, deep thud. My arm aches all of a sudden, but the smell of the peaches is worse. I might vomit.

"Deer," I say again, nearly breathless.

"Are you okay?" Pete reaches for me. I nod. He slides across the bench and pulls me into a tight, tight, too-tight hug. "Look at me." His hands on my cheeks, turning my face to his. "Are you hurt? Is your arm okay? Did you hit your head on the dash? Anything?"

"Are you okay?" I say, my words choking my throat before I force them out.

"I'm okay. I'm okay." He squeezes me again. "We're okay. We're not hurt. We're good. You're breathing too fast."

I nod. I know it, but I can't stop.

"Ants," I say with one short breath. "There will be so many a-a-ants."

"We can handle ants." Pete presses his hand to my chest. "Just slow your breathing."

"I—I—I can't. . . ."

He pushes harder. His hand there is almost as painful as the tightness in my chest.

"You're breathing too fast too." I put a hand on his chest.

"The deer," he says. "Is it still there?"

I don't want to look, but it's my job to do the broken things, injuries, bloody stuff, small repairs. Sometimes big repairs. That's always been my job. He has to sit down if he sees blood, no matter if it's a cut that doesn't even need a Band-Aid.

I glance out the window and see it right away, lying in the

bright light from the truck, clearly still breathing, even though it's otherwise motionless.

"What if it's not dead?" Pete says.

"It's definitely not dead."

"Does it look okay?"

"It does not look okay."

He groans, a sob catching in his throat.

"It can't move, but it's not dead?" Pete's voice trembles.

Just now I realize that the truck is on a slight angle. Looking around, I see that we are halfway up the berm. All the peaches have slid over to the driver's side.

"We need to go look," I say.

"What if it gets up and goes into the forest and it's hurt?"

It's not going anywhere.

I put my hand on the door handle. "Stay here."

I'll do this. I'll fix this. This is an Annie thing to take care of. Not a Pete thing. And not just because I eat meat and he doesn't, because it would be stupid to pretend it was that simple. And not because we argue about guns sometimes, and unlike him, I'm not totally against them. At all. I go hunting with my dad, but I've never shot anything other than empty beer cans filled with water, and cardboard boxes stuck on the fence with targets drawn with marker. When I go hunting with my dad, we never go into the forest more than an hour from the truck. He doesn't even bring a bottle of water for himself. Just a beer in each pocket, and a bottle of water and a chocolate bar for me in his pack. When he aims, he means it. He always kills in one shot. Every time. Military precision, because he was in the army.

The door is jammed shut. I stick my head out the window and see in the fading light that not only are we angled up the berm, but this side of the truck is sitting atop a wide, smooth boulder, and the door is crunched in at the bottom. Without a word, I climb over Pete and open his door, which swings away fast, wedging against the dirt with a crunch.

The truck is going to be a problem, but I don't want to say that out loud yet.

First things first.

"You stay here." I scramble out of the truck and up the little hill, out of the way of the truck.

The strip of dirt road and the forest on either side are shaded in dark blues, with the sky just a little lighter still. The air is cooler; there are no more shadows. The deer is lying in the middle of the road. Its front hooves move just the tiniest bit as I get closer, like that's all it can muster to try to get away.

Its eyes are wide open, wet with fear. Its nostrils flare rhythmically. There is no blood, but it cannot even lift its head as I get closer. It's so scared, but it can't move.

Behind me, I hear Pete get out of the truck.

"Annie?" Pete doesn't come any closer. "Is it going to be okay?"

I shake my head.

Pete vomits onto the dirt.

"Just stop breathing," I whisper. "It's okay to go."

Suddenly a ringing in my ears blocks out all the other noise. The deer, the wind through the trees. The crickets. Pete. Those are the words I said to Gigi moments before she did stop breathing.

I remember thinking I should smother her. Take a pillow and press it over her face, like she had asked me to do jokingly a month before, then seriously just before she stopped talking altogether.

I could smother the deer.

The ringing quiets, and all those sounds come back, louder, it seems.

"Annie?" Pete's beside me now. He kneels, reaching out, just about to touch the deer.

"Don't," I say. "You'll scare it more."

We should just go.

I turn my head and see that the truck is definitely not going anywhere. This deer is a problem, but the bigger problem is that we are here in the middle of nowhere, and the truck is screwed.

"We have to do something," Pete whispers.

"Or we could let nature take its course."

"The truck is not nature," Pete says. "The truck did not take its course."

It did, actually, with Pete driving. But I don't say that out loud, because of course he didn't mean to hit the deer.

◆ ◆ ◆

I can't smother it.

I can't break its neck.

I can't slit its throat.

I can't bash it with a rock.

"I wish my dad was here," I say.

"I wish he was too," Pete says. "He would fix this."

"But we can't, Pete." I take his hand and start backing away. I have to really pull to make him come with me. "We just have to go. We just have to leave it."

Could I slit its throat?

I'm thinking about this and untangling our packs in the back of the truck when I realize something. The smell of smoke is worse up here than it was down in Sedro. Pete looks up at me from inside the cab, where he's collecting our phones and water bottles and maps.

We stand at the back of the truck, the packs on the tailgate, stuffing everything where it belongs.

"There was a fire above Lake Shannon," he says. "I bet it's that one. And the wind just shifted or something."

"Probably."

There are already over a hundred wildfires burning in Washington, but while that sounds like a big number, it's not really. There were over six hundred up in British Columbia last year by the end of the season. Even now there are fires burning all over, but regular people hear about them only when they get close to homes and people get evacuation orders.

At Fire Camp, we'll get to go to one of those fires. Only a small one, like a lightning strike, before it has a chance to be much more than a little brush fire. But we'll be the ones to stop it. Our field supervisor on the trail project went to Fire Camp, and he told us that they say they keep the minors away from the front line, but he managed to get right up to the flames and beat the shit out of them with his own bare hands. That's what we're going to do. Tell the fire off and then murder it. Payback for destroying our forests, year after year.

I will toast to that. And so will Pete. I'll stick one vodka in his flame-retardant overalls and one in mine, or two, before we go to the fire, and when we kill it, we'll clink that plastic and raise a toast: *Take that, murderous beast of flaming doom*.

When we walk away, we skirt into the forest on the right, our headlamps illuminating the fat tree trunks, the branches like black wings overhead.

That's right, Annie. Think about wildfires.

Think about the smell of hot strawberries and smoke.

How those tiny red berries tasted when you pressed them against the roof of your mouth.

"Remember those strawberries?" I say.

"And the smoke."

I take his hand, so thankful that it only takes three words and we can go back. To another crazy night, and its strange, sweet finish.

◆ ◆ ◆

A few minutes later, we scramble off of the trail and back onto the road. The moon is only a crescent, so while it's bright enough out here to turn off our headlamps and let our eyes adjust, it's too dark to actually see anything beyond each other and the degrees of black and indigo blue that make up the wilderness on a dusky night.

"We're about ten miles south of the trail," Pete says.

"If we follow the road?"

He knows what I'm thinking. Why waste ten miles walking on a dirt road if we can cut in at an angle and follow our bearings northeast until we join the trail?

Neither of us wants to hike up a logging road.

Pete glances at his phone for the time. The screen is obnoxiously bright.

"It's almost eleven," he says. "How far do you want to go?"

"A couple hours?"

He nods.

I nod.

But neither of us moves in the direction of the forest.

Another long moment passes, and then we look at each other and know exactly what the other person is thinking. Without a word, we drop our packs and start running back down the road.

We see the truck first, and I think maybe the deer got up and walked into the forest, but no. As we get closer, I see it. Only now it's not moving at all.

"It's dead," Pete says. I can hear the relief in his voice.

"It is dead."

He takes the back legs, and I take the front legs. It's still warm, and for one second, I worry that it's not dead at all, and that we'll be stuck trying to fix this again, with no way to fix it. But no, it's dead, its head dragging, tongue lolling, as we pull it off to the side of the road and pile branches and rocks over it until it's buried.

When we finally crawl into our sleeping bags, I want to talk, about anything other than the deer, but Pete—this is always his solution to hard things he doesn't want to talk about—is asleep a minute later. I'm jealous that he can do this, if only because my not being able to leaves me with *hours* to overthink things. Which is another thing Pete doesn't do.

Right now I cannot stop thinking about the deer. Wondering if we should've left it. Wondering why we hit it in the first place. That poor deer. Pete's ruined truck. And we are in the middle of an unplanned nowhere because of it. And then I come back to the deer again, lying across the narrow track, illuminated by the high beams, its eyes searching for a way out that its legs couldn't execute. If I squeeze my eyes shut to stop thinking about that deer, I only end up thinking about when my mom hit a deer.

I hadn't seen her for almost a year when she turned up one school night when I was twelve. Pete was sleeping over because his dad was leading an expedition up Mount Rainier. He tried to stay close after Pete's mom died, but he was still away a lot. Pete was already asleep beside me, covers thrown off, his pajamas twisted around his scrawny torso. His earphones under his chin, and his audiobook playing along without him. I remember trying to guess how long he'd been asleep so I could put the book back about that much, because it mattered to me even if it didn't to him. Pete can happily drop in and out of a story, but I have to read it or listen to it from start to finish, without missing a word. He was listening to the same book that I was reading, and I didn't want him to miss any of it.

I piled my book and Pete's iPod and earphones on my bedside table and headed to the bathroom. I was standing in front of the sink, brushing my teeth, and then suddenly she was in the doorway behind me, and I saw her in the mirror like a ghost, only I didn't jump. I didn't scream. I just held my toothbrush in midair, like a wand or a weapon, the white spit trickling down my wrist.

She put a finger to her lips and shook her head.

"They don't know I'm here," she whispered. "This is just a surprise for you."

She came into the bathroom and shut the door behind her. And locked it. Even with the door closed, I could hear the movie from Gigi's room. Dad was in the basement tying lures, with one of his political thriller audiobooks on.

She sat on the edge of the bathtub, patting the spot beside her.

I wiped the toothpaste spit off my face and put my toothbrush back into the ceramic mug with my name on it.

"You know your Gigi made that for you."

Of course I did.

She stared at me for another moment and then patted the edge of the bathtub again.

"Sit, Annabella."

"Annie."

The outline of her was so stark against the pale green of the bathroom, it was like someone had carefully drawn around each contour of her with a black marker. She looked like a cutout from a magazine stuck onto a background of my house. Like a paper doll. Only, she was talking. Slow at first, and then faster.

"I bet you're surprised to see me. Right? Right? Did you wonder where I've been? Did you write letters to me?"

I hadn't, but now wondered if maybe I was supposed to.

"Doesn't matter," she said. "What matters is that you love me. I know it, letters or no letters." She laughed. "But, but." She laughed harder. "But! A letter would've been nice."

"I didn't know where you were," I whispered.

"You could've written them and saved them for me for when I came back."

"I didn't know you were."

"Coming back?"

I nodded.

"Maybe you just need something to write those letters to me in." She grabbed her big purse and set it on her lap and dug deep for something she was having a hard time finding. "Let me fix that. I got this for you. It's perfect. I know you'll love it. I saw the cover and I thought of you right away, you know? How that happens sometimes?"

"Does Daddy know you're here?"

"I walked right in, didn't I?"

"Does Gigi know you're here?"

"She's got her movie on." She pulled out a diary and handed it to me. "Perfect, right?"

I flipped it over to see the cover.

A unicorn, midleap over a shimmering full moon, the night sky behind it, each star a tiny sparkle.

"Do you love it so much?" She pulled me into a hug. "You do love it so much. I can tell. I remembered that you love unicorns."

"That's Pete. He loves unicorns, not me. I don't love anything."

She stiffened. Stood. Said nothing. Then she snatched the diary back and shoved it in her purse.

"Let's go."

"Where?"

"I want to show you something." She took my hand and pulled me so forcefully that I had to stumble along behind her as she led me outside. Why didn't I call for my dad? Or Gigi? Simple. I did not want to go with her, but also, I absolutely did.

◇ ◇ ◇

Which is how I found myself riding shotgun in my mother's crappy old Toyota Echo, all dented down one side and with no rear bumper, heading west. She hadn't said much since the bathroom.

She had the radio on a talk channel, a call-in show about personal finances. Her purse sat between us, on the hand brake. The diary stuck out the top, the little stars sparkling whenever we drove under a streetlight.

"If you'd written me, you could've told me you didn't like unicorns anymore."

"Pete does. I never did."

"Well, good for Pete!"

"I like otters?"

She was driving fast, not slowing down for the curves, just cutting across them instead, and then all of a sudden there was the deer, standing in the middle of the highway, staring right at us as my mom headed straight for it.

"Mom!"

"It'll move."

"Stop!"

"It'll move!"

But it didn't, so she swerved to the left but hit it anyway, because it finally had moved, right into her path.

The car screeched to a stop. My mom gripped the steering wheel and stared out into the night, the pool of light from the headlights. The deer was behind us.

"Get out of the car."

I looked at her, not sure if I should do it, even though she said so. It seemed impossible, to get out of a car in the middle of the road, at night, in the middle of nowhere, with a dead or injured deer the only company for miles around.

"Take this." She handed me the diary. "And get out."

I didn't move.

She leaned across me and opened my door. Then she undid my seat belt and pushed me.

I got out, and before I could ask her what she wanted me to do, she drove off.

I was alone on the road.

There was no deer. It must've gotten up and run into the woods, but in that moment, I was sure it had vanished. Turned to particles of nothing and dispersed into the darkness. No way to be resurrected. And that I would vanish too, before anyone would find me.

I was only there a minute or two before my dad pulled up with Gigi and Pete. I got into the backseat with Pete, who was wearing his pajamas with his coat over top and nothing on his feet. Before he could see it and tell me how awesome it was, I dropped the diary to the floor and kicked it under the seat. Stupid unicorns. She couldn't even get that right. Pete was unicorns. Not me. I wasn't into anything in particular. Except rocks.

Crystals

The smell of smoke is stronger when I wake up, alone, our orange tent glowing and hot under what I guess to be a midmorning sun, which I can see overhead because we don't have the fly on. I smell smoke in the distance, hot dirt all around, and wildflowers, which I didn't notice last night as we crashed into sleep so fast after such a crazy day.

Pete is outside, far enough away in the alpine meadow that he could be a log or a rock; if it weren't for his rainbow unicorn trucker hat he has parked on his face to keep the sun off, I wouldn't know it was him.

Between us? A carpet of lupine and paintbrush and elephanthead.

"Hey!"

He sits up, then leaps up and runs my way.

"Sleep much?" he says.

I shrug.

He squats in front of the tent, where he's cleared the ground down to just dirt and set up the stove.

"Look!" He pulls a tiny flower from behind his back. "Purple saxifrage."

According to the trail maintenance camp last summer, this is very, very rare.

He puts it in the palm of my hand. "I found a little patch by those big rocks." He points. "Northeast, exactly. We'll walk right by it. I'll show you after coffee."

"Only if you brought that gross vegan creamer," I say as I stuff my sleeping bag into the sack. "Which is slightly better than no creamer at all. But not if it's vanilla! I hate that even more."

"Plain."

"I love you, Pete."

As we cross the alpine meadow and head back into the woods—moving ever northeast—the wildfires are definitely behind us. The sky is clear blue ahead, and just a thin haze back to the west.

Pine forest.

Mountain ash and alpine meadow.

Forest.

Alpine meadow.

Then back into more dense forest, where it's cooler, which is a relief. If it was midmorning when I woke up, it's probably midafternoon now. We never check the time unless we have a very good reason for it. The more you check the time, the slower it moves. And the faster your phone battery drains. Not that the phone would be good for actual phone stuff way up here, but it still makes a good backup compass, and, more importantly, Pete's has the topographical maps.

Trees, rocks, flowers, sky.

Trees, rocks, flowers, sky.

I say this over and over as I walk, because it is so nice not to be thinking of anything else.

By the time we stop to eat—call it lunch? Dinner? I don't know—we've started a list of the wildlife we've seen. Squirrels, marmots, chipmunks, groundhogs. A couple of black bears up a steep slope. And a stag. Which at first I was sure I was imagining, as if it were the protector of the deer we hit last night. But then it kept staring at me.

"Pete?"

"I see it."

I stir my bag of freeze-dried beef lasagna.

"Why isn't it moving, Pete?" I whisper.

"I do not know, Annie," he whispers.

It stares at us until there is a sudden loud crack from somewhere east of us. The stag bolts across the rocky meadow and disappears into the forest on the other side.

"What was that?"

"Maybe a tree falling."

"That was *not* a tree falling."

"Definitely not." Pete stands up.

"Wait!" I grab his arm and pull him down. We're both crouching, our foil bags of reconstituted food abandoned in the dirt. "You don't know what they're shooting at!" I whisper.

"They're not shooting at us," Pete says, not whispering. "They can't even see us."

"And how much bright orange are you wearing?"

None. Brown shorts, green T-shirt.

"You look like a tree, Pete."

"Well, no one wants to shoot at a tree."

"Whatever!" I flap my hands. "The tent." I start pulling it out, but there's Pete, stepping into the clearing and hollering.

"Hey! Don't shoot!" he shouts.

"Wait for the tent!" It's pooled at my feet, and I'm just about to unfurl it and wave it and be way more safety conscious than I normally am when we hear voices.

A woman hollers back at us from roughly where the shot went off.

"All clear!" she says, and then I see her. She looks like a tree too, khaki capri pants and a bright green tank top. She's waving at us. "Are you coming this way?"

I glance at Pete. "Want to?"

"Sure." He shrugs. "Might be the only people we see."

"Okay." I pick up our lunch garbage. "Only because I want to know what the hell they were shooting at."

✧ ✧ ✧

The woman in the tank top meets us in the clearing and leads us into a forest of fat pines, marching up the steep slope. She says her name is Paola, and she's from Seattle. We see a quad just above us, but no real track that it could've come in on.

"Ty can get that thing into pretty much anywhere," the woman says when she catches me looking at the filthy, bashed-up quad. "Do you know about this place?"

"This place?" Pete says.

"I'll take that as a no."

"What were you shooting at?"

"Our dog brought a bear our way," Paola says. "Scared it off."

"That dog is just a snack to a bear. A tasty morsel." I raise an eyebrow at Paola's polished nails—not very long, though—her makeup, the two ponytails of shiny black hair, and the push-up bra that is absolutely lifting up to the name. "It takes a special dog to know how to be a backcountry dog." Like the one we had until two years ago. Marble, who was such a good hunting dog that my dad didn't want to be disappointed by one that couldn't live up to Marble. But this was not a piece of small talk that I wanted to offer.

"Agreed. Spencer is not that special kind of dog," Paola says, which irritates me more than if she had argued with me. "He always comes back, though. So far. We know someday he might be a bear's amuse-bouche. That's a—"

"Tasty morsel," I say. "We know."

"Her dad cooks a lot," Pete says.

Spencer lets out a string of high-pitched little-scrappy-dog barks. He is tied to a folding chair and barely as big as a shoe box.

Never mind just bears. One time Pete and I saw a falcon catch a rabbit. We were watching the rabbit from the edge of a meadow. We hadn't even noticed the falcon until it swooped down, grabbed the rabbit in its talons, and swooped back up above the trees. We watched the rabbit dangling and twisting, until we couldn't see them anymore. That rabbit was bigger than this dumb dog.

"Baby?" Paola shouts. "They're here! Just a couple of kids, backpacking."

Ty pops up from behind the base of one of the bigger pines on the slope.

"I don't do the digging," Paola says. "I don't like that much dirt. But they're fine with digging in it until they're covered in it. You have to go under the trees. That freaks me out, but Ty doesn't get claustrophobic. They'd be good to go to rescue a toddler who fell down a little well."

Pete catches my eye—we're going with "they" pronouns for Ty, following Paola's lead. I nod.

Ty is big, with upper arms as thick as my thighs, so it's not likely that they could fit down a little well. Skin as dark as the loamy forest floor. They drop a pickax, grab a kid's beach bucket, and clamber up the slope with more grace than I would expect of someone who looks like they spend most of their time in the gym.

"Hey," Ty says. They reach out a hand. "Ty."

We all shake hands. Ty's is so dirty that Pete and I both have filthy hands when they let go.

"Wanna see?" Ty lifts the bucket, but when we both lean in to look, Ty pulls back for a sec. "But first we have to swear you to secrecy."

Pete and I glance at each other. "Sure," I say for both of us.

Ty lets us look in.

Hundreds of perfectly formed crystals. Only a few look like what you'd see for sale in a rock and gem store, but those are so clear and pointed that I can easily imagine them with a silver cap on a thin leather cord around my neck.

"You did not get those from right here," Pete says, clearly as awed as I am. "No way."

"Yes way."

"We sell them," Paola says. "As far as we know, no one else knows about this spot."

"So now you have to kill us after all?" I say, only half joking.

"Don't need to," Ty says. "You'll never find this spot again."

"We have our ways," I say.

"Sure." Ty shrugs. "But are you going to hike back anytime soon? Even if you do"—Ty does a royal flourish with their hand—"I grant thee rights to all the crystals you may find, in exchange for scaring you, and for getting here on your own two feet."

"Really?" I grab Pete's hand. "Let's stay and dig!"

"That is the best idea ever." Pete unstraps his pack and lets it drop, startling Spencer, who starts barking.

Paola grabs a stack of colorful buckets. She gives me the top one, then hands one to Pete. It has a unicorn jumping over a rainbow on it.

"Because of your shirt," she says. "And your hat. And your pack. And the pins."

"It's a thing," Pete says.

"Clearly."

Ty leads us down the slope, to a tree they tell us would be good to dig under. Before our trowels hit the dirt, we see that the ground is peppered with tiny crystal points pushing through. The sunshine that leaks through the trees catches each one, making it look like the forest floor is dappled in tiny, twinkling fairy lights.

After a couple of hours of digging, we've come up with a small pile of crystals, dirty and beautiful.

"Can you believe these come out of the planet like this?" I have five in my hand. Pete has another bunch in his hand. Our buckets have even more, just not quite as beautiful as these.

"Unreal," Pete says.

"Says the unicorn," Ty says.

"Not an insult," Pete says.

"Not intended to be," Ty says. "Hey, do you know what a unicorn is?"

"I do know how to use the internet." Pete blushes.

"Good to hear."

"I've got a girlfriend."

"Fair enough."

I look from Ty to Pete and back. I think I'm missing something, but I'm not sure that I want to look stupid.

"We should get going." I grab Pete's arm. "Thank you so much. This has been so amazing."

"Like being on another planet," Pete says.

"You know what I learned from Pete?" I say as I gather my things. "Unicorns were first mentioned by a Greek doctor in the fourth century BCE. He was wandering in the woods and came across a single-horned ass."

"A single-horned ass!" Ty laughs.

"Correct," I continue. "But really, most people think of unicorns as a biblical animal. Holy."

I stop babbling so that we can say goodbye and get on our way.

I sigh when we are well out of earshot.

"Biblical?" Pete asks.

"You told me that!"

"I don't think most people think of unicorns as biblical."

"So, what do they think?"

"Like, what they meant?" Pete says. "Back there?"

I nod. Repeatedly.

"It's stupid."

"You only say 'It's stupid' when it's totally not."

"Okay, fine. A unicorn is a third in a couple. There."

"Like a plural wife joining a marriage."

"No, not like that."

And then I get it. And I get why this is so awkward and I

should've left it alone. Pete and Preet, sexual partners. Add Annie, sexual partner to them both. Annie the *unicorn*.

"Which none of us are thinking about, so shut the fuck up." I buckle up my straps and walk fast in what I hope is the right direction.

"Nope!"

I angle more to the left.

"Nope!"

I spin around. "Then get your shit together and show me the way!"

We decide to camp just above the slope, right where they parked the quad. We're tired from hiking and digging, so as soon as we put up the tent, we decide it looks so comfy and get in it. We talk about Ty's pronoun preference as we take the cards out to play a game of Uno, which we don't even finish, because we fall asleep with seven cards still held in our hands, which works for me, because I do not want to discuss unicorns anymore. Not for a long time. And definitely not in relation to couples and the treasured, elusive unicorn, which is not me. I am not a unicorn.

I wake up in the middle of the night. Pete's awake too, his arms behind his head.

"Tons of shooting stars," he says. "So bright I can see them through the netting."

I sit up, tidying the cards back into the little waterproof bag we carry them in. "Why are you awake?"

"Couldn't sleep. I sorted my crystals."

Smallest to tallest, cloudy to clear. I touch the sharp, glassy tip of the most beautiful one. A scepter about half as long as my pinkie, cloudy with tiny shards of purple amethyst at the base, then not another blemish. It didn't even need to be washed.

"That one is for Preet," he says.

"She'll love it." I set it back down in its place.

"Why are you up, Annie?"

Not because I was dreaming of Preet and Pete and a unicorn.

"I had a dream the fire was coming."

"It does smell stronger. What if it gets too close?" he says, but then he shakes his head. "No. It can't move that fast. We're fine." He takes the cards from me and tucks them into the lid of my pack. "Come on, let's sleep outside." He chases me out, giving me just enough time to shove my feet into my shoes.

While I shrug on my fleece jacket, he collects the sleeping bags and mats, the sacks full of laundry and spare clothes we use for pillows. He sets up our beds just outside the tent, where it's still flat. He lays his bag atop his mat and climbs in. "Shooting star. There."

"Did not." I wriggle back into my bag.

"Did."

I see one too, right away, arcing across the sky all bold and bright at first and then thinning into invisible.

Pete's arm is under my head, just how I love it. Our sides touch, from shoulder to calves. These sleeping bags zip together, and I want to tell him we should, because why not, it's almost cold.

But I don't say it.

And neither does he.

Not because we both know that I am not the unicorn, but maybe because we're both thinking that Preet might be.

"It's stupid, what Ty said."

"Stupid."

"We're us," I say. "And you and Preet are *Pete and Preet*."

I can feel him nod, but he doesn't say anything.

"And unicorns are the thing that makes you better than the other guys. Because you're you, and you like rainbows and sparkles and painted nails and feather boas just as much as you like rock climbing and working on your truck and fighting wildfires."

He's asleep. I wish he weren't, because with the silence come my own thoughts, and being alone with them isn't always the best thing. I fall asleep and dream about wildfires and unicorns and Preet, striding through the flames to walk right between Pete and me, no matter how often I squeeze my eyes shut and move us farther and farther.

Uglier Mug

The sun is a dark orange this morning, but Pete and I aren't worried. Besides, it's not like we can really go back, because this is day three and we're just about halfway to Loomis, where we'll come out and phone Fire Camp for a ride for the last twenty miles. Once we can charge our phones. Lots of people would hitch the rest of the way. But not us. We made a pact to never do that again. Also, we don't know where the wildfires are. The smoke is everywhere. Worse to the west, yes. But also thickening to the south. The north is clearer, but there's a mountain right there, which means we'd have to hike straight up to go that way. Like, an elevation of nine thousand feet in less than five miles.

It's clear to the east, and that's where we're going, so there is nothing to worry about. The fires don't scare me. They're like bears. Give each other a wide berth, that's all. It's been smoky all summer for the last three years. If we waited for clear skies to do anything in the wilderness, we'd never do anything at all.

After about three hours of hiking, we come to a rushing creek and, beyond that, a field of snow that shouldn't be there, considering it's June. It's covering the trail for as far as the eye can see. Neither of us is wearing proper hiking boots. We never do. Always approach shoes. Kind of half hiker, half shoe. Lighter. Faster. And not waterproof at all.

"I'll see how it holds." Pete gingerly takes one step and ends up sinking to his knee. "Crap."

"Crap." I help him out, hurriedly untying his shoe and dumping out the snow and shaking out his sock before the snow has a chance to melt. "That's not going to work. Our shoes won't ever get dry again, no matter how long we park them beside a fire."

Damp feet equals bad news.

"Barefoot?" Pete suggests.

This isn't as odd as it sounds. Pete and Everett do a lot of barefoot running, so his soles are as thick as hide. And always dirty. Sometimes he shoves his gigantic feet in my face just to drive me nuts. It works.

"I don't want to."

"Might have to."

"That's a mile at least!"

"You can do it," he says. "Easy peasy, Annie Bananie."

"But my feet are so pretty and tender."

"Only compared to mine, maybe. If you want to see pretty feet, look at Preet's."

As if I haven't. Either she gets a professional pedicure every month, or she's really good at doing them for herself. If we were actual friends, I'd ask her. But we're not. We're Pete bookends. We should have team shirts: *No, I'm with Pete!* An arrow pointing one way. *No, I'm with Pete!* An arrow pointing the other way.

Pete powers up his phone. "I need to plug this into the charger," he says as he moves, aligning ourselves with the topo maps. "Hmm."

"Are we lost?"

"Nope." He glances up, smiling. "What we *are* is close to the hot spring I told you about. We weren't going to go north for another five miles, but we can angle up from here. It's two miles south of the PNT. And we're about four miles south of that, so we'll angle up to it."

"Whoo-hoo!" I start running along the creek, doing a little dance. "Let's go find a hot spring!"

We hike for hours along the creek, on a trail that isn't a trail at all, or not for humans. It's an animal trail, nearly carpeted with grassy pucks of cow dung from the range cows, wet dollops of bear scat full of partially digested berries, and millions of round turds of all sizes, from moose to rabbit—and, if I were to get down on my knees in all that shit and really look, mouse and vole and shrew too. All the shit.

"We are literally walking in shit," I say after an hour of silence. "Do you remember when Gigi fell into that pile of manure my dad had just dumped by the garden? She really was a serious drunk."

Pete is deep in thought. He doesn't hear me, or he's pretending not to.

"We should sing something," I say. "Scare off the bears."

Nothing.

"Because some of this is bear shit. Look at all those huckleberries and grass in it."

Pete just trudges along ahead of me.

I stop. "Pete!"

"Huh?"

Gigi always said that Pete is a very skilled ruminator. I think we were about ten years old when she said so for the first time. "Perhaps because of the tragedy he experienced at such a young age," she'd say. "Yes, yes, you too, darling Annie, but Pete is more sensitive than you. You are a pouter. A grudge holder. But you do not ruminate."

"I promised Gigi that I would make you better."

"This is making me better."

"I feel like this hike is your one chance, you know?"

"No, I don't know."

"Okay, maybe it's me. Maybe I think that, and so I want you to get it right," he says. "This is the hike where you kick your own ass, Annie. Because Gigi isn't here to kick it. If we leave this up to your dad, you're going to still be living with him when we're thirty, and he'll still be making you salads from his garden and getting you to feed the chickens like you're still a kid. And then he'll say, 'Banana, you go ahead and do what you need to do.' Just like he does now. Annie, seriously. Seriously. So, so seriously. We're members of the

Dead Mom Club. We know how to do life better than other people, right?"

"When my mom died, Gigi didn't get out of bed for a week."

"Fair."

"And when she did get out of bed, she spent a month in her satin pajamas and kimono."

"Did Gigi flunk eleventh grade because she lied to everyone?"

"She left school when she was fifteen."

"Did Gigi have a mom like yours?"

"A good, pious Christian woman who knelt on sugar to pray."

"So, also crazy." Pete sighs. "Play along, Banana. Let's make the most of this trip." He reaches into his pocket and brings out a candy, stuck in its wrapping. Unicorn Whatsits that Preet brought back from England en route home from India after spring break. You suck on them and they turn your tongue a surprise color. Red, purple, blue, orange, green. "Truce?"

"Truce." I unwrap the candy and pop it into my mouth.

Unicorns aren't Pete's thing just because he swears to this day that he saw one behind an abandoned hospital on a mountain outside of Zagreb when he was five years old and backpacking with his parents. That's when he started collecting them. And maybe that's when he started to *be* like a unicorn in a lot of ways, because by the time I met him when we were seven and he was starting school for the very first time after being homeschooled, he was already kind, and strong, and always wanted the best for people. He didn't care that people teased him because he couldn't read yet. He'd still cheer on the worst bully to get his best time in track and field.

Ty and Paola don't know anything about unicorns. Not real ones.

As we climb toward this hot spring, I can't stop thinking about my mom. One of the last times I saw her was when she came to pick me up and take me to a hot spring she'd heard of off Stevens Pass. I was ten. She wouldn't let me bring Pete, so I was in a foul mood. The hike in was kind of like this, but she was bounding up the steep hillside, tripping and laughing, being the version of her that was great, until it wasn't.

We'd parked late, and it was a two-hour hike in. She was practically running along the trail, and I couldn't keep up with her.

"Where's your energy?" she shouted from a plateau above me. "Get moving! We're not allowed to be up here after dark."

It was private land, and the owner gave permission for people to be on it only during the day.

"Hurry up!" she shouted when she was so far ahead of me that she looked like just another stump.

"You're going to wreck this!" she screamed at me when we finally found the hot spring. "Look at all this beauty all around, and here you are so lazy and slow that we're not even going to have five minutes in the pools!"

Two pools, parked at the edge of the cliff overlooking the valley. She wanted one all to herself, so I took the smaller, cooler one. We went in naked—she hadn't brought suits—and I was so worried that someone else would come that I could hardly appreciate how stunningly special it was to be there with her on the side of a mountain like that, as the sun went down, pulling the jagged horizon into a cool, blue darkness.

Pete and I walk for miles, mostly in silence, until we get to where the hot spring should be.

No hot spring.

"Pete," I say. "Where did you hear about the hot spring?"

"My dad's friend. He hiked down to it from the PNT a few years ago."

"A few years?"

"Maybe a lot of years," Pete says. "But he was really specific. Okay, so it's not exactly right here."

"Or over there." I spin. "Or there, or there."

"We'll find it."

"Or we won't."

"Annie," he says, and the way he says it, I know he's got heavy things to say. I want to plug my ears. I want to hike all the way through without stopping and start fighting fires, because he got that part right. That's what I need. Heat and flames in my face, death slapping my cheeks, and me with a shovel, my muscles aching, digging a trench and hoping the fire won't jump it. I don't want to think about anything else right now. I don't want to think about Gigi, or my mom, or hot springs. Other than how we didn't find this one.

"Can we just focus on the fact that there is no hot spring, and no stink of sulfur to lead the way?"

"The smoke is so bad we might not smell the sulfur."

I bump him. "The smoke is so bad and I can still smell your nasty stank."

"I love you too." He pulls me into an exaggerated hug, emphasis on his sweaty, hairy armpits. "Do you love me?"

"Not your pits."

He kisses my forehead, holding me against him.

"I'm sorry," he whispers. "I don't want to be your jail keeper. You know that. I would do this hike with you anyway, even if it wasn't an intervention to get you back into your life."

"I'm sorry that I still kind of want to wallow."

He kisses my forehead again, and that's when my body betrays me, and maybe his is betraying him too, because I feel the pressure of him against me, which sends a hot shoot of longing to every last capillary in my body.

He pulls away, turning his face so that I can't see his red cheeks. So I didn't imagine it. There is something there, from him to me.

"You failed a year of *school*," Pete says. "And you lied about it. You lied to Gigi about doing the work I brought you. You lied to your dad. And now it's caught up to you."

"I don't want to go back."

"Do it online, then."

"You sound like my dad," I say. "I don't want to do it at all. I told him the same thing."

"You have to, Annie. So you can get into college. So you can get a decent job."

"That's *you*, Pete," I say. "Maybe I just want to quit school altogether and get a real-life education. Now let's go and get back on track for real. As in, right now."

Right away I step in a giant, soft pile of bear poo, almost purple with berry remains. Ahead I see more fresh bear poo. Big bear poo. Really big.

Grizzly. In the area.

"Pete?"

"Yeah?"

"Grizzly shit."

I imagine a bear, constantly on the move to stay ahead of the fire. Looking over its shoulder at the flames slithering up a hillside not far enough away. Us, between the bear and the fire. The fire winning. A disaster big enough to knock Gigi's death to the side for a while. Something hot and dangerous, chewing up forests and sending the animals running for their lives. The smoke so thick they have to close the highways. Everything impossible to ignore.

The trail really is too narrow to walk side by side, but I walk so close behind Pete that I keep bumping into his pack. Our bear bells jangle, but whether or not they are effective is up for debate. Pete is wearing our big can of bear spray on his belt, but still we sing stupid little-kid songs, because whenever we get into bear country, we can't think of an actual good song to sing.

"My eyes are dim, I cannot see, I have not brought my specs with me."

We're hardly singing. Shouting, really.

But then I hear it.

Wuff, wuff. In the forest, just to my right.

"It's in there," I whisper.

We know that we aren't supposed to run away from a grizzly, but we speed-walk so fast that I bet we clear five miles in one hour, trying to put some distance between the bear and us.

I can hardly breathe by the time we get to a small clearing with no fresh grizzly scat. I down the rest of the water in my bottle, and so does Pete. We're still close to the river, so we find another animal trail to the shore. The river is fast and wide and deep and clear, but we use our water filter system anyway. All it takes is one bout of giardia for a person to swear off not filtering water. "Look over there." Pete points across the river. There is a narrow meadow with bright green grass butting up against one of the prettiest little rock faces I've ever seen. Even from across the water, I can see how I'd go up.

"How do we get across?"

"I think I saw a really wide shallow spot about a mile back."

"Totally worth it," I say. "We can keep going northeast along the other side."

So we turn around and head back, away from the grizzly.

◇ ◇ ◇

The water is not deep, but I wouldn't say it's shallow. We take our shoes and socks and pants off but put on the lightweight sandals that we bring every time we hike. They have a strap across the back and two across the foot, so they're good as water shoes too. Right now, though, I can't look away from Pete in his boxers.

Pete, who puts every single muscle in his body to work, and it shows. Pete, who has the best ass I have ever seen, in real life and anywhere else. His boxers are a snug fit, unlike his other ones, so I can see the bulge at his crotch, which puts a hot rock of something in my gut and reminds me of our one and only kiss. True to Pete, the boxers have unicorns wearing party hats on them. I want to say something about a party in his pants, but even my thoughts are stuttering, so I decide not to. I step into the water, my pack balanced atop my head.

"Oh my god, that's cold!" I tighten my grip on my pack. "Those new?" I actually do know what underwear he has, so these are probably from Preet. They look like the kind you buy at REI for thirty dollars a pair.

"From Preet. We were in REI together and she saw me looking at them."

"So! Cold!"

"My dick is going to freeze and fall off." He sucks his breath in as the cold water hits his crotch. *"Fuck."*

"That rock face better be as good as we think."

"That trail we were on was shit anyway."

The icy water is waist-high now. We both keep focus on the rock face, long with shadows now. It must be late afternoon. I'd glance up to look at the orange sun, but I don't want to slip, and I do want to get across as soon as possible, because I can no longer entirely feel my feet. But at least all the heat in my gut and the tingling throughout my body have succumbed to the icy water for now.

The little rock face is even better than Ugly Mug, if only because no one has probably ever been here to climb it. We decide to stay in our underwear so it will dry quicker.

"And it shall be christened Uglier Mug!" Pete hollers, his arms spread wide. "And it shall be good! And gnarly! Gnarly good. Full of gnarly goodness."

"Just climb already!"

"*You* just climb already!" Pete chases me to the base. "Do it. Come on. Show that shriveled little arm of atrophied doom who is the boss."

Turns out my arm is the boss.

"I guess there is a reason for the physiotherapy the doctor ordered."

"Just try hanging from your fingers a bit," Pete says. "Boulder down here."

Pete turns his hat backward and scrambles up one way, then another, trying a new line each time. All those muscles he puts to use crunch into action. He looks like an ad for the company that made his high-tech underwear. The smoky forest behind him, the late-afternoon shadows. I dig my phone out and turn it on. This is too good not to take a picture. My battery is low, and by the time I take a couple of pictures and a very short video of him scaling up to the top, it's on red.

"Pete!" I call when his feet are on the ground again. "Quick before my battery dies." He puts his arm across my shoulder and we grin. When we look at the photo, we notice the blood-orange sun just over his shoulder, as if it's resting on it. And our faces, tanned and totally filthy.

"One more," he says. He lifts my phone and eyes it as he poses to kiss me on the cheek. What if I turn right now? What if I just turn my head? The phone goes black. "That's okay. Grab mine."

I dig in his pack. We hear it before we see it. It's playing an *Outside* podcast. The one about the man who almost died after he was stung by hundreds of bees when he disturbed them while he was out in the wilderness by himself.

"Why are you listening to *Outside*? It's all so worst-case scenario."

"I couldn't sleep last night," he says. "So I listened to a couple."

"Well, now you have twenty percent battery."

"The charger is in the electronics bag."

Which is inside the waterproof bag. And it is. But no red light comes on.

"It's not charged."

"I charged it," Pete says. "Ask my dad. I had it on the kitchen counter. Overnight." He takes the portable charger and turns it over in his hand, as if a *TRY AGAIN* button will magically appear. "Okay," he says after a moment. "We'll keep my phone off until we need the topos. That's fine. Just won't have pictures or music or podcasts. We'll survive."

While Pete goes up one last time, I make sure we're not leaving anything behind, other than this perfect climbing spot in the middle of the extra nowhere that is the original middle of nowhere.

Pete looks like a cover of *Outside* magazine.

"The mighty unicorn!" he shouts before getting ready to scramble back down along the steep but doable slope just to the side of where he was climbing. He hops down to a little ledge—not even two feet down—but just as he lands, he bends over, grabbing his leg.

"Ow! Shit!"

"Pete!" I drop my pack. "Are you okay?"

"Yeah!" he growls through a clenched jaw. "Yeah. Just a scrape from a bush . . . a stick." He snaps it off and throws it down. The same dimensions as a half-used pencil. No bigger.

"Is it bleeding?"

He nods as he eases down the rest of the way on his butt, one hand clutching his leg. I can see blood oozing between his fingers.

"I'll get the first-aid kit." His is always within reach, kept in the pocket under the lid of my pack, because Pete gets queasy at the sight of blood, and so he figures if the kit is in my pack, he won't have to do anything with it.

I meet him at the bottom, and he's wincing, his eyes squeezed shut. "Don't be a baby," I say. "Show me."

He takes his hand away and turns his gaze to the sky. His happy place. He's imagining that he's flying, or maybe BASE jumping, or paragliding. Flying a plane. My happy place is the water, his is the sky.

"Tell me," I say as I press my bandana against his leg and hold it there as firmly as I can.

"BASE jumping," he says. "From the top of a mountain, shrouded in fog. Then I run off and I'm flying along a narrow valley, and it's clear now. Blue sky. White clouds." I sit on the dirt and lift his leg into my lap. After a few minutes of pressure, I take away the cloth, fully expecting the bleeding to have stopped. It's slower but still bleeding a lot. The cut is deep. That half-pencil stick must've dug in deep and then torn up about an inch.

"Pete—"

"It's fine." But he hasn't looked at it. He's still looking at the sky.

"You need stitches."

"I don't." He looks at me at last but avoids his leg. "Let's cross back to the other side of the creek—"

"With your leg like this?"

"Annie, I didn't look at maps for this side. We're almost out of battery, so we can't look at them as often as we'd need to on this side. I know the peaks and the lakes on the north side. I know what the land is supposed to look like. We're already so far south of the main trail, I've got to use what we've got, which is a little bit of phone and a lot of my memory."

"Not until it stops bleeding."

"No." He shakes his head. "Let's just cross right now. Before we don't."

He moves my hand out of the way and ties the bandana tight. He hobbles to where the packs are and lifts his onto his head. I follow him and do the same, and then we're getting into that same icy water and doing the trip in reverse.

I wish we'd never crossed in the first place.

Pete drops his pack as soon as we've stepped out of the water. He collapses onto the nearest boulder and winces, the look on his face so twisted with pain that I suddenly have the urge to cry.

"Are you okay?"

"Translucent wings," he says, nodding. "No rainbows. Too corny."

This makes me laugh. He is a lot of corny.

"Can you look now?" He waves at his leg.

The water did slow the bleeding, but I rip open an alcohol wipe. The wipe is dry. So is the next one. And all the other ones we have too. I dig in my pack for the vodka bottles. Pete doesn't even give me a dirty look as he opens one and downs it. I do the same.

"Ready?" I open the last five and line them up.

He squeezes his eyes shut as I empty the first bottle on his wound.

"Ow! Shit! *Ow!*"

One after another, until the bottles are empty.

"Hold still."

I sprinkle anticoagulant powder on the wound before trying to pull it together with Steri-Strips, but the gouge is deep and sloppy, and the strips just don't stick. I put some sterile gauze on and wrap the whole thing with the Tensor bandage, because I am sure nothing else will stay put in the middle of his calf.

"Tighter," he says. "It's not going to stay."

"We can't wrap it too tight, Pete." I start to feel a little shaky inside, like this is a bigger moment than it seems.

"It's okay, Annie." He smiles at me, genuine and confident. "It'll be absolutely fine. Remember that wilderness first-aid course we took?" He leaves my bandage but puts his bandana over top too, tight.

"Yes." That feeling has gotten louder, a ringing in my ears. It's just a small cut, I tell myself. Pete was top in the class and walked away with a gigantic first-aid kit for the truck and a small one that's in his pack now. He knows what he's doing. Theoretically.

In practice, he can't handle blood, or even the thought of a bone poking through skin. He literally goes pale if anyone gives any detail about any gnarly injury. He passed out when his dad sliced open his forearm with a box cutter last year and he had to help him with it, and then he passed out again when he saw blood all over our new trail shoes, which were in the box Everett was opening. They still have stains, even though Everett did his best to wash the blood out.

"I promise you . . ." He thinks about it. "Okay, I promise you three things. The wildfires are going to stay out of our way. We are both going to love Fire Camp. We are both going to be official fire slayers by the end of the summer, and then one more year and we can do it for money." He winces as he gets up. "That last statement doesn't count. It's an addendum to number two. Third, now that we're back on this side of the creek, we *are* going to find that hot spring."

"Let's forget about the hot spring. Let's just keep going, okay? We're already a day behind."

"We'll count the crystals as a half day."

"And cutting in farther south because of having to leave the truck."

"We've pretty much made up for that."

"And now this!"

"It's nothing, see?" He puts his full weight on it. "It's not too bad."

"Pete."

"Annie."

"We're having this conversation in soaking-wet underwear, with your leg bleeding from a gaping hole."

"Small gaping hole."

"I'm just saying that I get it, and you can stop. *We* can stop."

"Stop what?"

"The Great Annie Rescue," I say. "You got me out. Out of my rut. Out of my house. Out of my head. Out of my grief, okay? This can just be a hike now. It doesn't have to be a movie."

"Out of your grief?"

"Well, maybe not that. But out of my head, which is the main thing, right?" That's what always scares him, that I'll get stuck in my head like my mom did, and everything will unravel. "I am officially out of my head, so long as you don't count me worrying about your leg."

"My leg is fine. It was just a plot point so you could focus on something in the real world. And it worked. Roll credits!" Pete stares at me, smiling. For a moment, I can imagine that the cut on his leg didn't happen, because his smile is all Pete, no pain. "I missed you, Banana. You had me worried."

"I missed you too, Unicorn Pete." I point to his leg. "You still have me worried."

"Totally fine."

"To be worried?"

"My leg is totally fine."

"Stay here." I poke around the edge of the forest until I find a tall, sturdy stick that Pete can use to help him walk.

When I return with it, I see that he has something in his hand. Those boxes, from Preet. For the record, I do not want Preet here in this moment.

"Preet told me to take these out when you came back." He hands me one.

From my own mess, he means. Not back from getting the

stick. Even though I would not be surprised if she could foresee the whole trip, as smart and intuitive as she is. Aggravatingly talented at knowing what people need before they need it. What's in the box, for example. Without even opening it, I know that it will be expertly perfect in every way.

"What is it?"

"I don't know." His box has a two on it. "We're supposed to open yours first."

When I lift off the lid, I see a note folded inside. Even before I unfold it, I know who it's from. It smells of Chantilly. *Gigi*. That smell makes my heart crunch in on itself, and I have to wait a moment before I can take a full breath again. The tiniest, most ridiculous thought occurs to me, that she might be there, right behind me, if I turn around. Of course she isn't. Even if it were possible, the only wilderness she experienced was picking blackberries along the road.

"I don't get it," I say. "What are these? What is she doing?"

"Preet didn't tell me."

The note is written on Gigi's special stationery, with roses all around, and pale pink lines. I read the letter out loud. "'Dear Annie and Pete: A gift to you from beyond the grave, or the ashes, so to speak. Take care of each other, my dears. Love, Gigi.'"

It's a thin silver chain with a unicorn pendant, no bigger than a bottle cap, with *Soul* engraved on the back.

Without a word, Pete opens his and finds a matching unicorn, with *Mate* written on the back.

Neither of us says anything as we clasp the necklaces

around each other's necks. What can I say right now? What can I say that won't sound flippant, or shallow, or so deep that I can't climb out of it? What do you say when your best friend's girlfriend gives you a message from your dead grandmother? It's too intimate. Or weird. Or so much of both that there is nothing to say about it. Don't make it too big, Annie. I touch the necklace that now rests at my throat. *Soul.* Pete touches his. *Mate.*

You don't have to say anything at all, Annie.

Oh, but I do. And what I want to say is this: Did Preet know what was inside the boxes? Did she and Gigi have a conversation about how Pete and I are soul mates, which means that she is *not*? Is this a concession?

I give my head a little shake. A few short seconds to myself to let my thoughts run wild, and I come up with this being a gentle and elaborate way for Preet to break up with Pete so he can be with me, his soul mate.

"Okay. We can go home now," Pete says. "Mission accomplished."

We both laugh, and keep laughing as we start hiking in our still-wet underwear, our clothes lashed to the outside of our packs.

Soul. Mate.

Soul Mate.

We walk away from the sunset, away from home, long shadows cast in our path. Pete isn't limping, so it can't be as bad as I thought.

Bear Creek Campground

JUNE 23

The best kind of day on the trail is when we both wake up in a good mood and have something to talk about. This morning it was all about what the hell I was going to do with my life, and for some reason, I was okay with it. Maybe it was because of the blue skies above, because the winds were pushing the smoke out of the way for once. Or that I'd saved the best oatmeal flavor combo for today—two plains plus one maple cinnamon plus one apple pie. If you close your eyes and imagine you're sitting at Thanksgiving supper with the football game on too loud in the background and Gigi lecturing Everett on how a meatless holiday is not a holiday at all, you can just, *just* about taste apple pie.

"That is such bullshit," Pete says as I try to convince him of this yet again. He's walking ahead of me. He may or may not know that I'm keeping an eye on his bad leg. "You need a crunch to give you the right texture. Not mush."

"That time I brought candied pecans and sprinkled them on top."

"Now, *that* was crazy-accurate fake pie."

"If we keep up this pace, we'll go farther than we have for days."

I watch his leg.

If I hadn't bandaged it and seen the mess myself, I would have no idea that he got hurt back there at Uglier Mug. But I know Pete. He plows past things that would stop other people in their tracks.

"Aren't you getting tired, Pete?"

"If you're talking about stopping for lunch, then yes."

"Mmm. Shriveled-up soy protein mock-chicken butter chicken."

"And rice," Pete says. "That's the best, Annie. Love that shit. Could eat two."

"We could swap for the lasagna? I get two of those, you get two of the fake *buck-buck*."

Pete stops in the middle of the field of boulders we've been making our way over for more than an hour. "Look!" He's pointing up. "Peregrine."

"Nope."

"Then what?"

"Wings are angled differently," I say. "That's a hawk."

"Or a frigging pigeon, if you're denying that it's a peregrine."

"Not a peregrine."

We keep weaving between the bigger boulders.

"That is a hawk."

"Is not."

"Is too."

"Isn't, Annie."

"That is a goshawk." The bird is almost right above us now, so I have to shield my eyes from the smoky red sun. "Look at the wings."

"That is a peregrine."

"Pete!" I chuck off my pack and root in the side pocket for the little pair of mostly useless binoculars. Sometimes I think I was born without the gene for using binoculars. Pete says they're fine, but I can't usually see anything in them other than a green mash of forest or all sky. But now I take my time and find the bird in the sky and get it into the best focus I can. "Flap, flap, glide. That is an accipiter."

"Pulling out the big words."

"Goshawk." The bird swoops toward a tree at the far side of the clearing and lands on a branch, giving me a perfect view. "Huh." I hand him the binoculars. "We were both wrong."

"Let me see." Pete looks and laughs. "Hello there, sweet little kestrel."

"Not a peregrine falcon."

"And not a goshawk." Pete lowers the binoculars. "But I was more right than you. Kestrels belong to the Falconidae family, Banana."

I shrug. "Still not a peregrine."

"Do you know what a group of kestrels is called?"

"Is this a joke?"

"No. For real."

I think of the other collective nouns that I know for birds. A murder of crows, of course. A flamboyance of flamingos, a parliament of owls. My favorite: a shimmer of hummingbirds.

"A congress?"

"That's eagles." Pete tucks the binoculars back into my pack and lifts it to help me get it onto my shoulders. When he turns with the extra weight, I see him grimace. I forgot about his cut and how terrible it looked yesterday. It cleaned up nicely, which gave me permission to forget all about it, apparently.

"Put it down, Pete."

"It's okay." He lifts my pack onto my shoulders. "I just turned funny and it pulled at it a bit."

"That's kind of gross."

"Kind of is."

"When we stop, we can put a clean bandage on it."

"Hover."

"A group of kestrels?"

Pete yanks my hat off and tousles my hair, which he loves to do now that he's tall enough to be confused for my dad from a distance. Or *a* dad, because my dad is not that tall.

"Let's head into the woods." Pete checks the compass. "We can get out of the sun for a while." He wedges my hat on top of his and takes off at a run. "Looks like you'll need some shade, seeing as some asshole stole your butt-ugly hat."

"Lucky fishing hat!" It used to be my dad's, and it shows.

Greasy around the rim inside, stained so much that it looks like it could be camouflage on purpose—coffee, sweat, beer, fish guts, chocolate—and decorated with fly lures he made that are so colorful and expert that birds sometimes swoop way too close to get a look.

That hat is like my backcountry teddy bear.

"Give it back!" I run after him and tackle him to the ground, which is a soft alpine carpet sprinkled with tiny purple flowers and wild strawberries that aren't ripe yet.

"Not so fast!" He keeps the hat just out of reach.

I straddle him, which is made very awkward because his pack is still on his back. He's like a turtle.

"Get off!" he hollers.

"Give me my hat."

"Not until you promise me that you'll graduate."

"Really?" I scramble off. "Forget it, Pete. My dad put you up to that, didn't he?"

"Not the hat part." Pete gets onto all fours and looks even more like a turtle. He hobbles a bit when he stands up to follow me as I walk away in a huff.

"You'll give it back," I say. "You know what it means to me."

"And I know what you mean to your dad."

"My dad, who used to trust me."

"Your dad, who you've been lying to this whole time," Pete says. "And me too."

"I'll get sunburned and feverish," I say. "Maybe I'll throw up all over you, and you'll have to give me rehydration salts and cut the hike short. All because of keeping my hat. As what, some kind of punishment for me telling you that my dad was fine with me not finishing the year, and telling my dad that you were bringing me schoolwork to do? Gigi was dying. I stand by what I did."

Something suddenly hits me square in the head. My hat. I glance back to see Pete standing in the middle of the vast alpine beauty, his hands on his hips like a superhero with a pack for a cape.

"You tell me when you've got it figured out, then, Annie." He starts walking toward me, limping a little. He sees me staring at his leg. "It's fine. Don't worry about it. We want you to worry about *you* for once."

"You and Preet?"

"Me, and your dad, and Gigi, and my dad, and Preet. And Principal Hazan."

"Okay, okay." I raise my hands in a truce. "Let's just pretend the stupid hat thing didn't happen."

Pete bites his lip. He literally *bites his lip* so he doesn't say the thing that I walked right into. *Sure, Banana, let's just pretend it didn't happen. As usual.*

The woods are cool and dim, with slices of smoky sunlight angling through the trees and making a patchwork on the forest floor. There is hardly any wind, so the trees are quiet and still, and we can hear so much birdsong that it starts to sound like that is what the world sounds like. Birdsong, and rushing water when we end up alongside a small creek.

"If I'm right," Pete says as he checks the maps on his phone, "I'm going to give you a surprise in about half an hour."

"I am not accepting surprises at this time," I say. "Please check back later."

"You'll want it when you see it."

A tall bluff of rock rises up to our left, and soon we are walking along a narrow ledge, with the creek far below us. There is a lot that I'd like to say about this part of the forest. But I'm not in a talking mood.

I hear it before I see it.

"A waterfall?"

"I don't know how big," Pete says. "But it was on the map."

The bluff rises even higher, and the trail widens, and then we see it. It's not big at all, but it is a bright, rushing promise of something in the middle of the quiet, sleepy forest.

"It's beautiful!" I drop my pack and kick off my shoes and make my way over the icy, slippery rocks to get close to the falls. The mist is a gift of cold perfection on my hot, sweaty face. "Coming?"

Pete shakes his head. "I'm going to sit for a minute."

"Not me!" I start peeling off my clothes until I'm absolutely naked. I don't care if Pete looks. If we're going to be together, then we keep our underwear on—an unspoken rule—but it doesn't matter if it's just one of us.

"It's colder than it looks!" Pete shouts over the noise.

I gingerly step toward the curtain of water, my arms over my breasts. As much as I don't mind him seeing me from behind, I don't want him to see me from the front. Somehow that's more intimate. Not *somehow.* It *is* more intimate. Everyone has a bum, but out of the two of us, I'm the only one with breasts and a vagina. *"Vulva,"* Gigi always corrected. "You see your *vulva*. You birth children and menstruate from your *vagina*."

I step under the water, and it's like a million shards of ice are raining down on my shoulders. I scream and leap out.

"Oh my god!"

"Probably comes from the glacier." Pete takes a handful of trail mix out of the bag and stuffs it into his mouth. "Cold, huh?"

"You didn't mention a glacier!"

He stares at me and chews through a big grin.

I'm shivering.

"Throw me my towel?"

He throws me my hat instead, and then my towel.

By the time I'm back in my clothes and eating my share of trail mix, the sun is starting to set, but we can't camp by the waterfall. There is too much mist, and all of our gear would get wet. So we hike another hour, feeling pretty proud of ourselves for making up some of the lost time even with Pete's bad leg, and then set up at the edge of another alpine meadow, by a party of hemlock trees that should give us some shade in the morning.

The smoke is as thick as fog and, as the moon rises, makes

the perfect backdrop for ghost stories. But it is also perfect for the kind of quiet that you get only when you're so far from civilization. So we do that instead. Quiet. We make supper quietly. We play two games of Uno quietly. Pete heads off into the woods with the orange plastic shovel quietly.

While he's gone, I look in his pack for his precious unicorn trucker hat. I'm going to keep it for a while as payback. Before I find his hat, I find an envelope sticking out of a book. I pull it out. It has my name on it, in handwriting that I don't recognize at first. The letter is sealed and very worn. Two of the corners are torn.

"Why are you looking in my pack?" Pete is suddenly behind me. "Do I need to defend my property with the little orange poo shovel?"

I stand, envelope in hand.

When Pete sees me with it, his face falls. That's what turns some very old gears in my head. All of a sudden I know whose handwriting it is.

"This is from my mother." All at once I want to rip it open and read what is inside and also tear it up or set it on fire and toss it into the hemlocks, no matter if it starts another wildfire.

Read it.

Burn it.

"Why is it here?" My breath catches in my throat. "Why do you have this, Pete?" He doesn't say anything, just has that disturbing look on his face. I know all of his expressions! "What is that face? What is that look on your face?"

"I didn't mean for you to just find it. I was going to give it to you."

"When? When were you ever going to give me this? That is mine! It's always been mine!"

"Gigi told me—"

"Gigi knew? No." I shake my head. "I don't want to have one single negative thought about her right now. Where did you get it?"

"I don't remember," he says. "Maybe I found it. It doesn't matter. I kept it for you. Gigi knew I had it, and she said to wait. And now she's not here to tell me to wait anymore, and she said I'd know when to give it to you—"

"It's still sealed! How did either of you know what's inside?"

"It's from your mom," Pete says.

"I know it is! You had no right," I say. "Neither did Gigi. It's not like this says 'Do not open until Christmas morning' or anything."

I rip it open. Just like that.

I know the look on Pete's face now. Absolute shock.

"See?" I unfold several thin, lined sheets of paper, the three holes on the wrong side when I turn it rightways to read it. The paper is covered in my mother's tiny printing. "Not hard."

In the dark, the cramped writing looks like a pattern on the paper, like it came from the factory that way. I'm not sure that I want to be able to read it, but Pete knows, and so he angles my headlamp down, focusing it on the paper.

Dear Annabella Georgia,

If you are reading this, then I did get to see you one last time.

I'm going to apologize, but first let me tell you a story.

Once upon a time, there was a mama unicorn with shimmering wings and a mane that threw off glitter whenever she shook it. That unicorn had a daughter, who was smart and funny, but whose wings were not strong enough to fly yet, no matter how badly she wanted to. So the mama unicorn carried her everywhere, showing her all of the beautiful things in the world. Rainbows, of course, and the aurora borealis. Music as glorious as the galaxy itself, and sunny days with blue skies, and campfires under the stars. Gazing up at the moon in all its predictable phases on warm summer nights, on a soft blanket, in a meadow, by a lake, at the foot of a majestic mountain. Swimming underwater in the ocean, in lakes, drifting down slow rivers on rafts made of lily pads. Jumping in piles of autumn leaves. Waking up in the morning to the smell of cinnamon raisin toast with cream cheese.

I can smell it again, right now, just as all those beautiful things in the world kick my memory, trying to make it remember, whether I want to or not. It goes on like this, a long, long, long list of the things my mother loved. Page after page after page of things that she *did* share with me, before she stopped taking her medication that last time. High tea, dogs with three legs, red licorice, funny typos, pretty dresses with skirts that spread way out when you spin around and around, bunnies twitching their noses, dark chocolate. Old movies.

Just like her mother, Gigi. Which was the only thing they had in common. Besides me.

Until one day, after a beautiful, beautiful, beautiful sunset of blushes and roses and lavenders and periwinkles, the mother unicorn and the daughter unicorn waited for the moon to rise up over the mountaintop. They waited and waited, until at last the daughter jumped up and pointed.

"There it is, Mama! So big and round and silvery bright!"

The mama unicorn looked where the daughter was pointing, but it was not there.

"Isn't it beautiful?"

It simply was not there, but because she didn't want to say so, she nodded. "It is so beautiful." Which she remembered to be true. But the night was dark and cold and scary and long for the mama unicorn, and worse, the sun did not come up for her either. She could see her daughter and everyone else living in warm, sunny days and cool, delicious nights. Light and dark, balanced and natural. As it should be.

But not for her.

The sun did not rise.

The moon did not rise.

The world stayed impossibly dark. So dark that there was no way to tell where the black sky ended and the blacker ocean began.

The mama unicorn knew it was absolutely true that if she stayed in the beautiful valley, this darkness unique to her would spread. She would get it on everything and everyone that she loved more than life itself. So she made the hardest decision of her life, to protect the small, bright heart of her daughter, who would never grow if there was no sun and no moon.

She would leap off the highest cliff and simply not open her wings. And in that manner, the world would be right and bright and dark in turns again, as it should be.

A cook who worked at the ecology center found her body pushed up against the dam three days after she jumped from the cliff along Highway 2, a two-hour drive away from our house, where I was asleep at the time, and so was Pete, whose dad still wasn't back from Mount Rainier.

For three days, I didn't know that she was dead.

That note was in the diary when she gave it to me in the car that night she took me. If I'd read it then, would I have understood? Would I have known what to do? I felt a surge of rage. How was I supposed to know what to do? I was just a kid who wasn't sure how much she loved her mother versus hated her.

"Are you mad?" Pete puts an arm across my shoulder. "I just

didn't want you to hurt anymore, because I know how hard it is to have your heart smashed. When I showed it to Gigi, she said the same thing. We didn't want you to hurt more than you already were."

"I'm not mad at you."

Later, Pete falls asleep and I lie awake, thinking about my mother. I read the letter twenty times. I try to be mad at Pete and Gigi. My dad would've wanted to see the letter too. They kept it from us! But even as I try to be upset with him and Gigi, I'm not. I would've done the same thing.

The Hot Spring

JUNE 24

I think I will dream about my mom, what with the letter tucked under my head and having read it over and over. Instead, I dream about the cabin I went to for the three summers when my dad was dating Naomi. It was her cabin, on Lake Shannon, near Concrete. It's not so much that I dream of the cabin, but of just one night over and over.

Gigi had already gone to bed, and my dad and Naomi sat on the beach, by the fire pit, the flames blinding them from seeing us as we slipped out into the water. We wore life jackets, but only to shove them down to wear like skirts when we got out to the middle of the lake so we could float sitting up. This was our greatest discovery of that summer.

The moon was just a sliver, hardly there at all.

Perfect for shooting stars.

We saw just two. Pete gave me the first wish. He took the second.

And then, as if just two shooting stars were all we had

been waiting for, we both started to shiver. The shore was impossibly far away. We could see the fire. We could hear Dad and Naomi laughing. We could've shouted for help, and any number of people on the beach would've come for us. But we didn't want to get caught.

"Never go in the water without an adult," Naomi told us every single time we arrived at the cabin. "Or you won't be setting foot in it for the rest of the trip."

We wriggled the life jackets to where they should be and started to swim.

Swimming was my strength, not Pete's. I could've cleared half the distance in just a few minutes by myself.

Finally, Pete stopped, flipping on his back for a rest. I flipped onto my back too and held his hand, like two otters not wanting to drift apart. That's when we saw the shooting stars. Three in quick succession. He closed his eyes, but he wasn't wishing.

"Swim!" I splashed his face. "Swim!"

When he didn't respond, I grabbed his head with both hands and pushed him under the water. I held him there while he thrashed and fought, and when I let him up, he was ready to swim. We sang "99 Bottles of Pop on the Wall" and were down to twenty-three by the time the shore was close enough. We stopped singing so my dad and Naomi wouldn't hear.

My dad still doesn't know about that night. He and Naomi stopped in our doorway on their way to bed. There were bunks, but Pete and I were both on the bottom, legs entwined, pajamas twisted. I woke when I heard their voices.

"So sweet," my dad said.

"Until she gets pregnant."

"It's not like that," he said. "These two are soul mates. That's different."

The way that we're sardined together in this tent, our necklaces read *Mate Soul.* I always sleep on the right. When the dream wakes me up, I can't shake how wrong it is that our bodies are in the wrong order, so I actually get out of my bag—no small feat, considering the tight mummy fit—climb over him, shove him over, and resettle on the left.

Now our necklaces look right. *Soul Mate.*

That's better.

Dreaming of the night Pete and I almost drowned makes me think of my mom, of course. She was alone. No soul mate.

She never had one. She couldn't. Her mind wouldn't settle into the calm a person needs to have the closest friends.

If my mother hadn't hit the deer, where would she have taken me?

Away.

It doesn't matter. *Away* would've been bad enough. Away from my dad, away from Gigi. Away from Pete.

After she died, I sometimes had to shove away a terrible kind of relief. Relief that she wouldn't try to take me again. But then that would be followed by an even more terrible sadness that she was never coming to take me away. That's a bad kind of tangle in the heart and head for a little kid. Even for a big kid too. I take the letter out again and unfold the paper. I fold it up. Unfold it. Fold it up, stuff it back into the envelope, and jam it into the very bottom of my pack. I won't burn it today. But I might burn it tomorrow.

Pete doesn't wake up at all, just keeps breathing deeply, his lips chapped, his cheeks so red that in the lavender-blue light of the hour before sunrise, I wonder how I didn't notice that he got so sunburned yesterday. I put the back of my hand to his forehead, which is also bright red. His skin is hot, and even though I know that he likes to sleep hot, I can't help but unzip his sleeping bag to his waist, because surely a person shouldn't be that hot when he sleeps.

I try to go back to sleep, but the birds get louder and louder until there is no way that I can sleep through it. The smoke from the Elephant Creek fire thickened overnight, and I wonder if the birds know something we don't. It's too hot to be in the sleeping bag, even though the sun is hardly up. Pete is still snugged into his. He's always cold. I roll over, face to face with Pete. His breath stinks, but I don't care. For almost six months when I was fourteen, we didn't get to have sleepovers because Everett was dating Victoria Who Owned the Tanning Salon, who figured she knew everything about being a parent even though she didn't even have a cat, let alone kids. She convinced him that we were having sex, and even though

Pete's dad believed us, and my dad believed us, Everett told us no more sleepovers. Thankfully, that rule only lasted as long as she did.

Victoria Who Owned the Tanning Salon clearly didn't understand one basic truth. If two people want to have sex with each other, they do not require a sleepover. Truck, car, any room in either of our houses, the backyard, several hookup spots at school, behind the baseball bleachers. These might just be places I've considered now and then, in that way. But Pete doesn't want to now that he has Preet. Even if he did want to, even just briefly, before.

I can say that he is my best friend, and I can also say that I wish we were more, even if that's the stupidest thing ever because it might "wreck our friendship," which always seems to be the problem in the movies. Or books. Or songs. Whatever.

I put my hand in the warm gap between his body and the bag at his shoulders. I would be lying if I said I haven't thought about sliding my hand into his sleeping bag.

I pull my hand back.

I've never done it because it never occurred to me before Preet asked him out. And now he has Preet, so I won't.

Honestly? I'm not even sure if I think of *him* that way. Sometimes I think it's my brain being stupid, and I tell myself that runs in my family. Don't do the stupid thing, Annie. Don't be like your mother.

✧ ✧ ✧

I stare at him, his sunburned face so close that I can feel his breath on my cheek. I can see the scar over his eyebrow from when he slipped on a big rock at the beach and smashed his head on an even bigger rock. He should've had stitches that time too.

We'd gone across a little inlet to look for agates and hadn't paid attention to the tides and got stuck, thus the need to scramble over the algae-slick rocks to get back to Gigi, who was already waiting to take us home. We were an hour late, which was her limit before she decided that we were dying, or dead. Hence the rush.

"Wake up?" I only whisper it. "Wake up, wake up, wake up."

I don't want to admit it, but we are way behind schedule. And with Pete's leg, it's going to take even longer to get to Loomis.

I get up and get dressed and get water from the creek and filter it into our pot and set up the stove.

The water boils in just a couple of minutes.

I find our mugs, add all the right ingredients in the right way in each of them, and stir. I crawl back into the tent—miraculously not dropping either mug—and hold his coffee close to him.

"Mmm," he says, a big grin on his face even before he opens his eyes.

"I love you, Annie Poltava." He takes the mug and carefully sits up with it. He winces.

"The leg."

"It's fine." He blows on the coffee. "You did perfect first aid."

"Maybe it needs stitches."

"It's got the Steri-Strips. It'll be fine." He grins. "It will make a great story to tell our kids."

Of course he doesn't mean *our* kids, the ones we'd have together. He means the kids he and Preet or whoever will have, and the ones I'll have with whoever, which I don't plan to have.

A great story to tell *our kids.*

He pulls out his leg, wincing as he does.

"Show me."

"It's fine," he says. "Promise."

He swings his legs into the tiny vestibule so he can get his shoes on.

I'm digging in my pack for my toothbrush. He peers out the flap. "Pretty smoky," he says. He focuses on his laces. "Where is it coming from?"

"Everywhere," I say. "West, mostly."

He gropes for the walking stick and helps himself up. I follow him out.

"You can't put your weight on it?"

"I can. See?" He hobbles a few steps. Yes, he's still putting some weight on it. But not much. The mint hot chocolate taste in my mouth becomes sour panic. This is worse than not good. This is bad. Very, very bad. All of a sudden I think about how stupid it is that I spent the morning mooning over him, as if actually *being* with him were ever, ever, *ever* an option, instead of figuring out how we're going to get out of this wilderness, with the edges burning ever closer.

"You can't hop the rest of the way, Pete," I say as we're eating our oatmeal in those same mugs a few minutes later.

"It's getting better."

I pull his leg across my lap. The outer bandana is crusted with dried blood and dirt.

"It smells."

"Just the dirt on the outside of the bandage. Mixed with old blood. It's fine underneath. Three layers of protection."

"I'm going to bandage it again." We carry only the minimal supplies for one trauma each, so I'll be using my bandages this time. The last of them.

"No." He pushes my hand away. "Maybe later. We have a few days to go, so let's not use yours until we have to."

I say nothing because I don't know what the right thing to do is. As I'm thinking about it, the wind picks up, and for a moment the air is just a little bit clearer. But I smell something other than smoke too.

"Do you smell that?" Pete says.

"Sulfur."

"The hot spring!" Pete grins. "It has to be close."

✧ ✧ ✧

If we find the hot spring, we'll be back on track. We can even connect with the PNT if we go straight north after. Then we could get help for Pete's leg or find someone with a sat phone. Pete is limping now, which is better than hopping. We pack up the tent and our packs and head toward the smell, which is conveniently northeast of us.

The smell gets stronger and stronger, and after just ten minutes or so of walking, Pete stops on the trail and points ahead, where wispy clouds of steam roll up and away from the pool, which we can't see yet. As we get closer, we see the pool itself, about the size of my living room, edged with small boulders slick with mineral deposits. The most surprising thing? No garbage. Even though people have been here. There's a little path to get in, two plastic chairs with their legs sawed short to use to sit in the water, and a couple of hooks drilled into the nearest tree, and beyond that is a shallow rock-lined ditch from the creek just above it, with a makeshift plug of rocks in a plastic basket at the top so you can control how much cold water is let in.

"Last one in is a rotten egg!" He drops his stick and his pack and starts running—well, hobble-running. I pass him easily, but he reaches out and grabs the back of my shirt.

"Cheating!" I yell. And then we're both down on the ground, and he's on top of me. It occurs to me that we end up like this way more often than best friends should. I want him to stay right there, long enough for him to understand that I can be better than Preet, but I throw him off, because as much as I wish I were Preet, I respect her even if I'm not. "Get off me, asshole!"

He rolls off, laughing, and jumps up, as best as he can, one-legged. Less than five seconds. He was on top of me for less than five seconds.

"Kidding," he says as he strips down to his underwear. It's the we-should-probably-check-if-we'll-be-boiled-alive-first moment.

Pete dips his foot in, while I go back a few seconds to when he was still on top of me. I draw out the moment. Imagine it lasts six, seven, eight seconds. He leans. Kisses me, just like he did last summer. No, even longer. Deeper.

Everything shifted a little after that. Not enough to push us apart, but just enough that I know that I still think about it and he doesn't.

"The water is perfect up here. Avoid that smaller pool below." He arranges one of the chairs in the shallow, silky pool but doesn't get in.

"Your bandage?"

"I'll take it off after," he says. "Mineral waters are healing, but the bandage will keep out the dirt."

Nine, ten, eleven seconds. His arms above my shoulders, the weight of him on me. A minute. That would be the longest time. Mostly, that's all I want. Just a minute to be that person to him. Not to push Preet away.

To be a unicorn?

I shake my head. No! Not like that. Don't be stupid, Annie. Don't you dare screw up the best thing in your life.

Like we almost did that night of the Orionid meteor shower, when we biked along the Cascade Trail to find a good dark spot above the Skagit River. It was late October, so Preet had already been at our school for six weeks, and Pete had noticed her enough that I was worried she would take him away. But that's not why the kiss happened. Pete lost the bet about how many stars we'd see in an hour, and he took it badly.

"You cheated!" He threw his hat at me. "You did not see three that I didn't see."

"I did!" I threw the hat back and tossed my water bottle at him too. "My three plus your one plus our six. Makes ten. I win."

"You saw two, maybe."

I shoved him backward and pinned him down. In that moment, I was thinking that I could see our breath, and that the ground was cold, and that if we didn't start biking back right then, we'd get shit from our fathers. But what I *did* was lean down and kiss him softly once, and then one more time, pressing my lips harder. He kissed me back, lifting his head off the ground to make it last longer because I was already pulling away. This could ruin everything. This could ruin *us.*

I could feel his erection pressing against me, and that's what scared me the most. He wanted this *too.* Even though that's not who we were. Who we are. What we need each other to be. I jumped off of him.

"It's late," I said as I shoved my things into my pack. "Did you charge your light? Mine's good. You can ride behind me if you didn't."

A very long, uncomfortable pause, and then he spoke, his voice catching just enough to give away that he was messed up about it too.

"Yeah. It's charged."

"Good, good."

"Yeah. Good." He turned on his light, making a narrow beam on the trail. "Annie? Maybe we should—"

"Should get going," I said. "We should."

So it was me who ruined what could've been. If I'd let it continue, if those seconds had become that minute, maybe we could've stayed like that.

A week later, Preet asked him out and he said yes. It took him almost another week to tell me, which was further proof that the night of the shooting stars was just as confusing for him as it was for me. It's the only thing he's ever kept from me, except for my mother's letter. Those two things are enough for a lifetime.

I peel off my five-day dirty clothes until I'm standing there in just my underpants and bra. Proximity rule. I know that my body is sexier than Preet's. She is lanky and bony and has tiny breasts. I have the body he wants. Or the type he always said that he liked, before Preet. A plump, round ass, a waist with curves, and breasts that he's told me are a ten. Even if that was two years ago when we found a joint his dad had left on the windowsill behind the washing machine, where he puts everything he takes out of pockets before he does laundry. We were looking for change, but that was even better. We both got super giggly and ended up talking about boobs. Lady boobs. Man boobs. *My* boobs. Also, important note: he was talking about them as a ten in general, not specifically for him.

"I speak for all humans who like boobs," he said. "You have very nice boobs, Annie Bananie. Banana boobs. Banana split. Want one?"

I step into the pool. It's so hot that I gasp, but then I sit in the wobbly half chair with the water up to my armpits and close my eyes and relax into the heat, so busy enjoying the deep, muscle-unknotting, tension-unlocking water that I don't think of Pete for a minute, until I hear him gasp. Gasp differently than I did. A painful gasp.

I see him, in just below his knees. Just above the bandages on his right leg.

"Hurts, hurts, hurts," he growls. "Hurts, hurts, hurts, hurts." He minces over to his chair and collapses into it.

"For someone in a hot spring, you're pretty pale, Pete."

"I'm going to throw up." He stands all of a sudden and tosses the chair out of the pool. He scrambles out and bends over, vomiting onto the soft blanket of moss and slime, then rights the chair and eases himself into it, his knees nearly at his chin because of the shortened legs.

All of this happens before I can even stand up, let alone get out.

"Pete?"

"I'm okay." He nods, eyes closed. "All good now."

I jump out, the quick movement making me dizzy. I lean over and brace my hands on my knees for just a moment.

"Pete?"

"That's me." He opens his eyes. "I'm fine. I just won't put my leg in."

I help him get his chair in a spot where he can just step in with his good leg and pivot and sit, leaving his bad leg propped up on the bank. I put my chair beside him and stick my legs out too.

"That bandage looks extra gross now," I say. It's sopping wet and bloody, sagging away from his calf.

"Good thing that I know you'll do a beautiful job of bandaging me up all tidy when we get out."

We had to drink all of our water just to get steady enough after the heat of the hot spring to get going again, and so then we had to set up the gravity filter and fill our bottles and bladders, which always takes longer than I think it will. Once we're ready to go, Pete takes out his phone to set a GPS waypoint for the hot spring so we can come back again. His screen is black.

"It's dead," Pete says.

"But how?" We've been so careful to turn it off after we checked the maps.

"I must've left it on at the waterfall."

"Okay," I say. "That's fine. We have the paper maps."

"I don't think we're on them anymore," Pete says. "We're still south of the PNT, but other than that, I'm not sure."

"Pete," I whisper, not sure what to say. "I don't have the maps on my phone. Because I didn't even know we were going."

"I *know.* I know. It's fine," he says. "We just keep going northeast. Loomis is that way."

"Northeast."

"North." He orients one outstretched arm. "East." Points the other.

"O"—I angle my arms in the same way—"kay."

We walk slowly, across steep slopes of scree that land us on our asses more times than I bother to count. Through forests dense with skinny pines that let the sunlight in like those blinds that hang vertically, half-opened. We move slowly because of the loose rocks and lack of trail, but mostly because of Pete, who hobbles along with his stick, which we tied a shirt to, bunched at the top, so he could use it as a sort of crutch too. Neither of us mentions how far we've gone. Or how far we *have not* gone. We don't talk about his leg. We don't talk about the wildfires, and how the smoke is thicker now, making us cough. Making our eyes sting. When we stop for the day, it's so late that it's almost dusk. As it gets darker, I keep scanning the edges of the steep ridge we just crossed, half expecting to see actual flames.

Not Lost

There's been only one other time when Pete and I were very far away from home and no one knew where we were. That was almost a disaster, but then it was also magical. To this day, the dads don't know about it. We told Gigi, but she was different. She was our secret keeper. Pete's secret keeper too, as it turns out.

Gigi was in charge, in theory only. She was an adult, yes. But we didn't need a babysitter. Pete was already sixteen and had just gotten his provisional license a week before. He wasn't supposed to drive with anyone under twenty, but we didn't care. Everett and Pete had been fixing up Luca's old truck for Pete, and it was in better working order than it had ever been.

We drove to the coast and then turned left, the misty ocean air and crashing waves on the right, the windswept trees leaning away from the weather on the other side. The skies were black and roiling with storm.

I had a satellite picture of the pullout we were looking for.

I kept my finger on the first landmark. A state park.

We zoomed past that, windshield wipers on high.

A creek.

Another creek.

A wayside.

Lighthouse B and B.

The orange bridge.

"There!" I pointed as Pete jammed on the brakes.

A narrow lane off the highway, and then a hill, descending into the dark toward the ocean.

"If we drive down there and it's flooded or there's some kind of supertide, we're screwed."

"There is a reason why the exhaust is up by the roof." Pete gunned it so hard that the unicorn bobblehead on the dash flew right off and into the little space behind the seats. He spun to a stop in the middle of a small clearing.

"Now we wait to sink," I said.

"It's not quicksand, Banana."

We were so eager to take Pete's new truck out that we'd already set up the back for sleeping, so we just hopped in, zipped ourselves into our sleeping bags, and ate the snacks we'd brought while Pete beat me at eight games of Uno.

I woke up freezing in the middle of the night, so I dug out my woolly hat and his. I snuggled Pete's on him while he slept or pretended to sleep.

Either way, when I lay back down, he pulled me to him, so

we were spooning in our sleeping bags. This was before Preet, when I still thought that maybe something would happen. I kept still, wanting him to slide his hand into my sleeping bag. But instead he started snoring and rolled away.

The rain had stopped by the time we woke up at dawn as two other cars pulled in, and then a truck too. Everyone headed for the beach with buckets and golf clubs modified with slotted spoons on the bottom. We were all there for the same thing. Agates.

Nobody actually made a run for it, but people did beeline for the beach pretty fast.

After Pete and I had each found half a bucket of amber-colored agates ranging from the size of a jelly bean to the size of a cherry, we ran into two old ladies. One of them showed us an agate the size of a goose egg.

Golden, with an oval hole on one side, and inside that, millions of tiny, sparkling bits of seaworn crystal.

"I found it five minutes ago, just up the beach."

The rock fit perfectly into the palm of my hand. It seemed to glow, even though there were black storm clouds above and no sunshine at all. The rock was translucent and its small cavern was pure magic. I slid my pinkie finger in and felt the absolutely ancient and microscopic landscape inside.

The old lady laughed. "Wave almost got me, but that's how you see them, isn't it? You're looking and looking and not seeing nothing, and then a pop of jewel right there and you just got to get it."

Pete nodded.

I nodded.

We couldn't look away from the rock.

I handed it back, very reluctantly.

"You'll need bigger buckets," she said. "If you want to take a good haul home with you. Lots on the beach after that stormy night."

"No," we both said.

"Just one really good one," Pete said. "Like that."

We found a Japanese license plate (which was probably tsunami debris, all these years after that terrible earthquake), a dead pelican, and a tiny waterlogged Bible. Very close to the Bible—fate or not—there it was. Pete spotted it first.

"There!" Atop an isolated big rock across ten feet of water. "Treasure." No one else was in sight.

"It's all ours," I said.

It was at least as big as the one the old lady had. It looked like a small Golden Delicious apple against the black rock.

"That, Annie Poltava"—Pete slung an arm around me—"*that* is our golden egg."

"How are we going to get it?" A wave rolled in, super close. We backed up as it smashed angrily just below us.

"I'm going to swim."

"No. You're not."

"Am so."

"Are not."

"Am so."

"Are not."

"I am!"

"Pete! No!" I pointed to the swirling water between the rock and us. The rising water. There was less than a foot between the golden orb and the water now.

Pete was already stripping off his clothes.

"Your dad is going to kill me, Pete!"

"You can tell him that his only child died doing something he loved."

"Not funny!"

"See you in a minute." He was down to his underwear. Then he stripped that off too and jumped into the surf.

I counted. One. Two. Three. Four. Five.

Then the undulating surface shifted, and I saw his blond head just below the even blonder agate. He reached up for it, but with the way that the water was rushing in and out of the tiny cove, he got swept to the left.

"Are you okay?"

I wanted to dive in after him, but of course that would be beyond stupid. Yet what else could I do, except collect his clothes so that I could help him get them on when he made it?

He swam against the tide, pushing his way back to the rock.

He reached up again, but this time the current shoved him forward, bashing him into the rock nowhere near the agate.

"Pete!"

"I'm okay!"

"You're not!"

"One more minute!" he shouted. "Just one more minute."

Maybe he didn't have one minute! He was too cold. The water was too wild.

Suddenly the two old ladies were behind me.

"What the hell is he doing?" the one with the agate said.

I was counting that minute. Thirty, thirty-one, thirty-two—

The other one shook her head. "Getting his rock, that's what."

"He's getting out," I said. Fifty, fifty-one. "Even if he doesn't get it."

"He'll get it," the first woman said.

We all stared. No one moved. Pete lined himself up one more time and pushed himself out of the water and made a grab and missed and made another grab and got it.

None of us cheered.

Pete didn't make one triumphant noise.

I could tell that he was too cold and too exhausted.

He swam back with slow, labored strokes. I could hear his teeth chattering when I helped him out of the water.

He didn't care that he was naked, or that the two old ladies were tsk-tsking him.

"Stupid!"

"Could've drowned. Then what?"

"Your girlfriend would've had to go tell your parents. Now, is that fair?"

"Put this on, you idiot." The one with the agate took off her fleece hat and yanked it onto his head, right down over his ears. "All the important heat goes out the top. Now let me see what this brouhaha was all about."

Shivering, Pete handed it to her. She compared the two. Pete's was bigger, but not by much. It was rounder, and the cave in it was bigger, with bigger crystals.

"Nice rock," she said. Then she wound up as if she were going to throw the first pitch in a Mariners game and chucked it back into the ocean.

"Babs!" the other woman said. "What the hell did you do that for? You damn fool!"

Pete stared at the spot where the agate had made the tiniest splash. I put my jacket over his shoulders, but it just looked like a little cape. He shivered, lips turning blue.

"Ignore my sister," Babs said. "Focus on me, kid. That was one of the stupidest things I've ever seen anyone do." She poked him in the chest. "And for a rock!"

"Which I worked really, really hard for."

"I'm teaching you a lesson. Do you know what the lesson is?"

"I'm pretty sure that you're going to tell me." His teeth chattered, shaking the words as he spoke them slowly through blue lips.

"I should get him back to the truck," I said.

"Putting yourself in danger is never worth it!" Babs nearly

shouted. "You could've died! And I'd've been here watching it happen. And my sister too. And your girlfriend would be scarred for life! How about that!"

"She's not my girlfriend," Pete said.

"Friend, then."

"*Best* friend," Pete and I said at the same time.

"Better a friend than a girlfriend," Babs said. "A fool like that is no keeper."

Babs's sister pulled her away, the two of them heading for the cars, which was probably the only way she was going to let it go anytime soon.

Pete watched the water for a long time, saying nothing. Then he shifted his gaze and watched the horizon for another long time.

"You're trying to talk yourself into looking some more?" I hugged him from behind to give him some warmth. "Or out of looking some more?"

"A little bit of both."

"You're too cold."

"I'm too cold." He nodded. "I'm too cold to keep looking. Right?"

"You're not going to get warm until you have a shower," I said. "And that is hours away."

Sighing, he took my hand, and we made our way across the rocky beach carrying our buckets rattling with tiny treasures. But not the big one.

✧ ✧ ✧

It started to rain halfway back to the car, proving that it was the right thing to have left when we did.

We took off our boots and crawled into the back and into our sleeping bags. Pete kept the pink-and-white hat on.

"I might never take it off," he said. "She was right. That was a stupid thing to do."

I scrambled between the front seats to look for the bar of chocolate that I thought was on the driver's seat.

It wasn't there, but in its place was Babs's golden egg. And a note.

This is an important moment.
I don't usually give anyone anything.
But I'm giving you this.
PS. I took the chocolate.

Pete's eyes were closed, but I knew he wasn't asleep. I took his hand and folded the big agate into it. He sat up right away, cupping the rock in both hands, the little cave looking at him. Then he started to cry.

"I think I almost died," he said. "I think I came really close this time, Annie. Really close. For a rock."

Keep Walking

JUNE 25

Pete is buried in his sleeping bag, turned away from me. Usually, he'd be up by now, so I give his shoulder a gentle shove.

"We should get moving."

He doesn't answer.

I reach to put my hand on his forehead, but even from a couple of inches away, I can tell that his fever is worse.

"Pete?"

Still no answer.

I shake his shoulder.

"So tired," he mutters. "Let me sleep."

"I can't. We're behind by a day at least, right? Not only can we not wait, but also we have to hurry. At least ten miles today. Okay?"

"Too tired."

"Where are we, Pete? Should we turn back? Would that be faster?"

He shakes his head. "Closer to Fire Camp."

I pull him onto his back. His cheeks are flushed, his eyes almost crusted closed with sleep.

"Open your eyes, Pete."

I'm not scared. I'm not scared. I'm *not* scared. This is not scary. This is going to be fine. Everything is going to be all right.

He tries to open his eyes, but they're too crusty, and he's too weak.

"Can't," he whispers.

"Try it again," I say. "Open your eyes." I stick my finger in my shirt and use it to clear away the crust. "There, try now."

His eyes open. A bit better, but he still looks like he's got a cloudy film over each eye.

"You have to get up, Pete."

"Let me sleep."

"Show me your leg."

"It's fine."

"Show me your leg right now!" I unzip the sleeping bag and fling it off of him. He's wearing only his underwear—unicorns wearing underwear—so I see right away that his bad leg is tomato red, with darker streaks, like an heirloom tomato, coming away from the bandages. He starts shivering but has no energy to argue. "I can smell it from here, Pete. Can you smell that?"

He nods.

"I'm going to look at it."

He shakes his head. "All good."

"Bullshit." I grab the first-aid scissors and cut through the bandage.

I see the wound and gasp.

The cut is oozing a viscous, cloudy fluid, and it's puffed up and bruised all around, like a sea anemone, as if it would tighten around my finger if I were to poke it. "You need to look at this, Pete." I let my hand hover over the wound, and the heat coming off of it warms my palm. "You need to understand how bad this is."

He wedges himself up on his elbow, but he still can't really see it, so I lift his leg, and he screams, so I put it down as gently, gently as I can. His whole calf is hot, and swollen too. He sits up straighter. I can tell when his eyes land on it, because he becomes very, very still, as if the leg were something that might bolt away on its own if he startled it.

"Shit." He whispers it. His face is pale as he whispers it again, and again. Over and over. "Shit. Shit. Shit. Shit."

"We need to turn back," I say. "We have to get you some antibiotics."

"We *have* antibiotics."

I dig in the first-aid kit for the bottle. The crossed-out label says that whatever was inside expired two years ago. Are these pills newer? I don't remember dumping them in.

"Did you put them in here?"

"You did." He holds his hand out for the bottle. "After reading that story about the guy who sawed off his own arm to get out of a slot canyon."

"They're expired," I say. "For sure."

"Better than nothing." He reaches for his water bottle, and even just that much movement makes him wince. "Give me two."

"Maybe three?" I say. "If they're expired, doesn't that make them weaker?"

"One." He takes another look at his leg. "It looks worse than it is."

He means that we need to save the pills so we have them to give him for the rest of the hike, no matter which direction we go. I realize that I don't know what's closer at this point. Home? Or Fire Camp?

"Do you think we're closer to home, Pete?" Suddenly the idea of it is an oasis on a burning horizon. My dad tending his tomatoes and feeding the hummingbirds. Everett running out to greet us wearing only underpants and the biggest grin in the world. "I miss the dads. I miss Gigi, even if she isn't there."

"I miss home too," Pete says. When he doesn't say anything more, I know what he means. He doesn't know where we are either.

I pack up camp while Pete lies on his mat outside, in the shade of the tree, his leg elevated on a rock. When I tell him that it's time to go, he says he feels better, but he's moving slowly and not putting weight on that leg at all, thanks to our makeshift crutch.

I nearly emptied his backpack into mine, cramming in as much as I could to reduce the weight of his. When I help him with his pack, he squeezes his eyes shut, gripping his crutch so hard that his knuckles blanch.

"Is that okay?"

"Did you take stuff out?"

"As much as I could," I say. "You've still got your clothes, mostly. And your sleeping bag. I've got everything else."

"Feels like you put in all your stuff," he says. "Just because I feel like shit doesn't mean you can get away with that, you know."

"Jig's up, then." I do up his chest strap. "We should get going. When is the last time you looked at the topo map?"

"With you."

"The day before yesterday, then."

"It's still northeast," he says. "That hasn't changed."

But we don't know what we're heading toward. Or the elevation, or how steep it is, or if there will be a river.

"You're sure it's not faster to turn back?"

"No. Honestly, Annie. It's not faster." His tone is firm. "It's way longer to go back."

This is when I know that something has shifted. I know this because I'm leaving things out. I'm not telling him that I'm worried about not having the topographical maps. I'm not telling him that I'm worried that the only reason we're not turning around is because we're so far off our original trail that even the compass wouldn't do us much good, or not any more than the sun and moon in the sky. I don't even want to tell him these things. I don't want him to worry more. I don't want him to think about the bad choices that got us to this piece of the wilderness that is so beautiful, with the river on one side and the mountains climbing up on the other, the sky hazy with smoke, and the sun like the plump deep orange grapefruit on the *Apocalypse Now* poster. Take a picture of this. I bring my hands up to my eyes like a kid with an imaginary camera. *Click*.

"Nice picture," Pete says. "Now let's go. I seem to be the only one carrying anything, so I'd like to get this show on the road."

By the time we start walking, it's easily noon, judging by that crimson sun.

Pete is walking so slowly that I don't think we'll even go five miles today, when we should be going at least twenty to make up for lost time. We were planning on fifteen miles a day to get to Fire Camp, with a day to spare. Now we're so far behind that I can quietly start to hope that the people at Fire Camp and our dads will report us overdue, and then we can wait for a helicopter. So long as we can get to the PNT. Where we're supposed to be.

Watching Pete walk is like watching someone limping through a different kind of atmosphere, where everything is heavy and thick. Clearly, there is no way he can go any faster, so there is no point in being a cheerleader. That's been over since yesterday.

Truthfully, I'm not sure that he knows what day it is. Or how far we are into the middle of nowhere.

"Let me take your pack, Pete."

"I'm fine."

"It'll help."

"I'm fine."

I reach for him, but he pulls away, teeters on his good leg, and then tumbles backward, landing on his butt.

"That moment in the movie when the main character . . ." I was going to say something about when the tough one is down but can't stand being weak and always protests too much and then ends up on their ass, humbled. Forced to accept help. A movie trope we've seen a dozen times or more. But this is no joke, and I don't make one.

"You okay?" I squat beside him. "Pete?"

He's propping himself up with his backpack, leaning against it, eyes closed, sun shining on his puffy red face.

He nods.

"You need lip balm." I am delighted to be able to do something, even this small thing. I pop the lid off and dab his swollen lips. He doesn't look like himself today. Not as in, *He's not himself today.* As in, he does not look like Pete at all. Put a picture of this person beside a picture of my Pete, and you would have a hard time believing that they were the same person.

"We have to go, Pete." I lean him forward, his shoulders hot to the touch. He's breathing fast, like a rabbit. "Let me take this."

He doesn't protest this time. I ease his arms free. He winces.

"What hurts?"

"Everything." He reaches for his water bottle. "Everything aches."

I wish I could tell him that we don't need to go any farther today. I wish we could just stay here.

"But we can't," I say.

"Huh?"

"We can't stay here."

"I know," he says. He says it again, in a whisper. "I know we can't."

"So let's go." There is a knot in my throat, which is how I know that I'm going to cry. I haven't cried about any of this yet, but seeing Pete on the ground, struggling to get up, I'm going to cry now. I offer him a hand and help him up. "We have to keep walking. Ever northeast, right? We'll find the PNT, we'll get on it, we'll get help, we'll get through this, and we will find this all really, really funny a few weeks from now."

"We can't go either," he whispers.

I pretend not to hear him.

He steadies himself with the stick while I arrange his pack on my front.

"Nice," he says with a grin. "That's a hot look."

"Right."

"You actually look really stupid, Annie," he says. "I'm being totally serious."

"You actually are really an asshole, Pete."

He starts to make the *L*-for-"loser" sign on his forehead but changes it to a unicorn horn at the last minute.

I do the same.

"Walk, Pete."

He tries to take a step. He can't even touch that one foot to the ground anymore.

"I'm sorry, Annie."

That's when the tears come. He's hopping down the trail ahead of me, wincing as he goes. At first I worry about him turning around and seeing me, but I can tell that he's so focused on moving forward, there is no way that he's going to expend the energy to stop and look back.

I don't frighten easily.

But I am terrified right now.

If I'm being honest, I might say that I am the most frightened I've ever been.

Before now, I was afraid of Gigi actually dying. Her being sick was almost easy compared with that. We had a routine. I did what I needed to do, and she did what she needed to do. We still had each other.

Before that, I was terrified when Gigi was diagnosed.

And before that, I was terrified of my mother. Not that she'd come back, because I always hoped that she would. I was terrified of her coming back to take me with her, which she did.

✧ ✧ ✧

Pete is slowing down. I count the seconds between one step and the next. Two seconds. Three. Four, for a long while. Now five. Five full seconds.

Then he stops altogether and turns to look at me, his face dripping with sweat.

"How far have we gone?" he says.

"How about a rest, then some more?" I put my hands on his shoulders. "We could go at least another mile like this. It's okay to go slow. It wins the race, right?"

He shakes his head.

"Just one step at a time?"

"Nope." He sways toward me, so I brace his shoulders to keep him up and steer him toward a rock just off the trail. I park him there, where he leans forward, his hands on his knees, his head down like someone deep in prayer. I kind of wish he were, because at this point, I'm ready to believe in God if it means Pete will get better and we'll get out of here.

"I don't have anything left," he whispers. "I feel like there's a hole in me and all my blood drained out, like there should be a trail of it behind me."

"You do have a hole," I say. "In your leg."

"Different kind of hole," he says. "Like a bleed-out you see in one of Gigi's crappy horror movies from the 1970s. Like when the man gets shot in *Karate Girl* and takes ten minutes to die."

"We're not talking about dying."

"Which is maybe still better than being eaten by a *Tyrannosaurus rex* while you're sitting on a toilet."

"In the dark."

"In the rain," Pete says.

"It wasn't raining."

"Yes it was!" He lifts his head at last, and he's smiling. I feel the first moment of relief in a long time. I hug him, but just quickly because I don't want him to know what a big deal the smile is, and how it means so much more than just the shape of his face in the moment.

"Wasn't."

"Was."

"Walk some more?" There's a lightness between us, and I think it can move him forward down the trail, even if it's just another mile. "Let's come up with a hundred cheesy movie deaths, and then we'll stop for another rest."

We start at one hundred and go down. One person describes the death, the other has to name the movie. All those hours of watching the Movie Classics Channel with Gigi after school should make this a breeze.

"Frozen in a hedge maze," Pete says.

"*The Shining.* Too easy." I scroll through the hundreds of cheesy movie deaths I've seen. "Oh! Got one. Iocane powder."

"*Princess Bride.* Stupid easy. How about . . . wood chipper."

"*Fargo.* Come on, Pete. I am the natural-born granddaughter of the world's most die-hard movie fan. Now one for you. Swallowing a pill that makes you blow up like a balloon and—"

"And then float up into the air and explode," Pete says. "*Live and Let Die.* 1973. Roger Moore as James Bond."

I can hear how tired he is, like there actually might be a trail of blood behind him, and I am glancing at the dirt as if it could be there. I *know* that his wound isn't bleeding. We need to keep walking. We have to go as fast as we can.

"Give me one, Pete. Come on. A hard one."

He takes a long time to think of one, his steps slowing as he does. He comes to a complete stop and then turns. Sweat drips from his nose and chin, and he's breathing like he's just run five miles. But he's smiling. He wags a finger at me.

"Bee stings."

"Candyman." That's not the movie he means, but I'm not sure why he's bringing up the movie that he does mean.

We have an unwritten rule with this game. He doesn't bring up movies with allergy deaths, or ones that will make me think of my mom, and I don't ever bring up movies that might make him think of his mom, who died in a way that is hard to believe, even for a movie.

I know exactly what movie he's really talking about.

"Sorry, Annie. It just slipped out. I don't know why I even thought of it. I know it's off the list."

"It's okay, Pete."

I don't want to talk about *My Girl.* A boy and girl, best friends. He dies after getting stung by bees. We watched her die not even a week after Pete had to use the EpiPen on me. Something occurs to me for the first time ever.

"Gigi *knew* about the bee sting," I say. "That's why she put that movie on for us when she did."

"You're probably right," Pete says. "That was her style. Leave it to Hollywood to teach the biggest life lessons."

"You and me on either side of her, bawling our eyes out at the funeral scene."

"Open casket, no less."

"Let's play a different game," I say. "Let's do foods, alphabetically."

"Can we just rest here a minute?" Pete says.

Seven words. Said lightly, even. But I know Pete. I know the meaning behind his words. It's not just about taking a drink of water or eating some peanuts and raisins. He means he's done for now. Full stop.

I bet we haven't gone two miles.

Day Seven

JUNE 26

It's just after dawn when I wake from the sleep that I thought I'd never fall into. I sit up and look out, across to where the creek is. I can't see it, though. The smoke is playing tricks. Hiding the mountains and making it look like we're sitting in a field, rather than a little valley between peaks. It looks like we'd just disappear into the smoke if we kept walking. If Pete could walk at all.

I roll toward him, still in the warmth of my sleeping bag. I'm going to unzip his and get a look at his leg, and then I am going to make an executive decision. Forward. Backward. Try to summon help right here. Something. Some *action*. Sanctioned by Pete or not.

He flinches when I get close. "No!"

"You have to show me."

"Wait, Annie. Just wait. Okay? Not yet?" He squeezes his eyes shut as he tries to roll away from me. He groans in pain.

"Let's just pretend the day hasn't started quite yet. Let's pretend that we're still asleep. Did you have a dream?"

"No. Come on, Pete—"

"A nightmare?"

"Pete—"

"I had a dream about my mom."

Now, that's not fair, because of one of our mom rules. Don't bring up the other one's mom, but if one of us wants to talk about our own, then we drop everything else. I sigh.

"I'm listening," I say. "Even though I can smell your leg from here. But go ahead."

"It was the same one."

His favorite day with her. He's lucky that is the recurring dream he gets. Mine is so boring that when I realize I'm dreaming it, I try to get it to change into something more exciting. Actually, Pete's is kind of boring too, but in a very sweet and special way. Precious normal, not boring.

"But it was a little different," Pete says. "This time she took me with her."

"Down the hall?" I don't like where this is going. Literally.

"It was summer, twilight. Still hot. My dad was in the hammock, me and my mom were on a blanket, shelling a mountain of peas we'd picked. 'Look up, Pete!' She pointed to the sky, where a thousand starlings were swooping and soaring together, like a celestial giant was painting swaths of peppery black, only to have them shift into another shape, and another, not a bird out of place." Pete's eyes are still closed, but his face has softened. "'Do you know what that's called, Pete? A murmuration.'"

I wait for him to tell me more, but when a very long time—just a minute or two, but it feels long—goes by, I decide that he's not going to, and that's okay.

"It's time to get up, Pete. We have to wash your wound. I'll boil some water."

"She was wearing that yellow dress with the white dots," he says.

Even though the dream is pretty much the same every time, what she wears is different sometimes. This dress is often in the dream, and it's the one she wore to his tenth birthday party, so I know it.

"Then she got up, with the bowl of peas tucked in her arm like a baby, and gave me a hand up and kept holding my hand. She walked us up the porch and past my dad, who raised his beer in a little salute. We went into the kitchen and put the peas on the counter."

That's the end of the dream.

Usually.

"Then what?" I say.

"She put her hands on my shoulders and said, 'You'll help me, won't you?' I nodded. Then she took my hand again and led me down the hall to the bathroom."

In real life, Pete was at school when she went into the bathroom to clean the tub just a week after his tenth birthday. She mixed bleach and ammonia together and died from the fumes. Pete found her in the bathroom, halfway between the bathtub and the door. His dad was just behind him, but she'd been dead for hours, and there was nothing he could do except take Pete out to the front stoop and tell him to stay there while he phoned the police.

Pete didn't stay there. He ran the three blocks to my house, curled up on the couch beside Gigi, and put his head in her lap, while *The Big Sleep* played in the background—Gigi never, ever turned the TV off, even when she slept—and I asked question after question.

"Did you get hurt, Pete? What happened? Where's your dad? Where's your mom? Are you okay?"

Right now Pete is very not okay. Maybe the most not okay he's ever been. But he is not going down the hall to the bathroom with his mom. He's not *that* not okay. That's completely ridiculous.

"I can smell it from here, Pete."

"Pretend you can't." His voice is strained. Exhaustion. Pain. His body doing the heavy work of fighting off the infection.

"I'm going for help." I can hear the fear in my voice. "I'll get search and rescue. They'll fly you out."

"You'll get lost."

"We *are* lost."

"We're not. We're heading northeast."

"Shut up about northeast! Northeast! Northeast! It's not doing us any good! Let me go ahead at least. You stay on this bearing and follow. I won't go off this bearing."

"Two of us out here? Separated?"

"Then we keep going together," I say. "I can lash a stretcher together with the backpacks and a couple of branches. With all our straps."

"I'm too heavy," he says with a little smile. "That would work if you were the one whose leg smells like death."

My heart fills with liquid ice. One tap and the whole thing will crack apart.

"It doesn't smell like death!"

"Rotting flesh, then. Which is exactly what it is."

"You really can't walk?" I whisper it, as if that might mean it's not quite true. "Not at all?"

He shakes his head, sure of himself.

"Okay, then. Fine. I can work with that. I can. I really can. I'm not just saying so either. I can get us help. Where are we?" I dig the map out of his pack, and the compass.

He sits up, wincing, and spreads the map on his lap. He moves his finger from the trailhead we were meant to hike in on, and all along a yellow line, to an intersection at a river.

"That's the PNT."

Then he moves his finger down and over, tapping a tiny blue dot.

"There it is." He laughs. "I bet that's the fucking hot spring. It was on the map the whole time."

"It doesn't matter now," I say. "Where are we?"

He moves his finger along the creek we're following and then stops about two-thirds of the way from where we started to our endpoint.

"We're somewhere near here."

"And by 'near,' you mean?"

"Give or take ten miles."

So we officially have no idea where we are.

It's hard to tell by the lines if the terrain between here and home is easier than the shorter distance between us and Fire Camp now. We are days away from anything in either direction, and the only people we've seen were Ty and Paola driving off on their quad, with their dog yapping and a wake of dust billowing out behind them.

He can't walk.

He can't walk.

He can't walk.

And we are in the middle of nowhere together, which I normally love. I love it so much. Except for this one time. I hate the endless dark forest, the rushing rivers, the rocky path, and the stupid hot spring Pete should not have gone into. Neither of us has said that yet. But I know it's true, and so he's got to know it too. The hot spring was probably full of bacteria.

Bacteria that has now devastated his leg.

I won't say it. On the off chance that it hasn't occurred to him.

I hope it never occurs to him that if he hadn't insisted on finding the hot spring, he'd be fine. And before that, if he hadn't fallen. And before that, if he hadn't planned this trip.

And before that, if I hadn't ground to a halt and needed him to get me actually living my life again.

And before that?

"Well, you just have to walk." I say this loudly. "We have to make you a better crutch, and then we go. As fast as we can. At least to the river, Pete. I can find my way from there. Then I can go get help once the map makes sense."

"No." And then, as if he has something to prove, he leans over and vomits between the sleeping bags. Retching and retching, with hardly anything coming up because he's hardly eaten for over a day now. With each thrust of his body, he lets loose with a terrible, low groan.

I pull his sleeping bag out of the way, and when I catch sight of his calf, I almost vomit too. It is cooked-lobster red, twice the size that it should be, yellow pus soaking the edge of the bandage. So is his knee, and his ankle and foot. There is no way he could even put that foot into his shoe anymore. Heat peels away from the leg as if it's a roast that Dad just took out of the oven. And the streaking. The thing that means trouble.

There's a word for it.

I put my hands on my knees and think hard.

What is the word?

Pete whispers something.

I half hear it, but that's all I need to remember the wilderness first-aid course we took last year. With Preet. I was so distracted by her being there that I got high in the bathroom on the first break and only half paid attention to the discussion on sepsis.

That's what it is.

Pete is *septic.*

Septicemia.

I don't remember much about it, except that for every hour that a septic patient isn't treated, the likelihood of death goes up by 8 percent. I can't remember if you're supposed to pull at an angle to remove a tick, or how to do a proper chevron with a Tensor bandage for a sprain, but I remember that statistic, and now I very, very much wish I didn't.

Does that mean that he's already at 100 percent?

Does this mean he *is* walking down the hall with his mom?

No!

No.

We'll call right now his hour zero. Diagnosis. Because if I think that he's already going to die, I don't know if I'll be able to do anything other than sit here with him and cry until he does or we're both consumed by the wildfire, whichever comes first.

A realization just a moment later: I remember why the detail about septicemia stuck with me. It was the story that the instructor told about a man who was scratched by his cat on a Friday, just before he and his wife were going to go camping. They got to the trailhead, he vomited, and they both decided to turn back. Saturday he had a fever and chills and spent the day watching soccer, and he was so bad on Sunday that his wife wanted to call an ambulance, but he said he was fine, and then on Monday he didn't wake up. He was swollen and red and hot, and his toes and ears and nose were turning black, and his pulse was racing. The instructor was the paramedic who picked him up. She said it looked like someone had boiled him and just taken him out of the pot. He was that red and swollen and hot to the touch.

Just like Pete.

I reach for Pete's wrist. Hot. So hot.

I feel around until I find the strong thumping. His pulse is racing.

"What was the ending of that cat scratch story?" I say. "I don't remember."

"He didn't die." Pete reaches for his water bottle and takes a sip. There's hardly any left. I'll have to go get some. Keep him hydrated. "He was in the hospital for months, and he lost parts of his arms and legs."

"And his ears and nose."

Pete laughs.

"You'd finally be as ugly as me," I say.

"Because you are so ugly?"

"So ugly."

I kiss his cheek, my lips still warm from the touch when I pull on my shoes and take out the water bladders and bottles and filter.

"Don't die while I'm gone, okay?"

"Okay," he says. "I'm looking forward to not having a nose. That'd be epic. At least Preet would still love me. You can't say that about many people."

I unzip the door, every ounce of muscle in me not wanting to leave him.

"Annie," he says.

I scramble back to him. "Do you want me to stay with you?"

He starts to shake his head, but I can tell even that hurts.

"We need water," he says. "And I want you to take the compass and orient us. Look for tall peaks, big water. Maybe we can figure it out from there. Find the trail again. There's a road at the bottom of the trail, on the other side of a river that we have to cross. We can try and figure out exactly where we are if we find that."

I want to ask him. But I don't want to know the answer, so I don't.

How far away should that river be? If he and I were practically running down the trail? If I knew exactly where I was going? I am so thankful that I can run.

"I'll be right back."

He reaches for my wrist. "You need to figure out exactly where we are."

He takes his hand away.

My wrist is hot.

"I think we should go back to the stretcher idea." I crawl toward the door. "Because I'm not going to go without you."

◇ ◇ ◇

The big creek—which could also be called a small river—is down a shallow slope, so when I get to the water and turn to look back, I can't see the tent at all. If you took a picture of me right now, you'd think I was all by myself.

"But I'm *not,*" I say out loud to myself. "I'm not. I'm not. I'm not. Pete is with me and he's going to be fine and I'm going to be fine." This is just another thing we survive. I park the filter bag, the bladders, and our two bottles on a big, flat rock at the water's edge. I'm going to collect the water from a few steps in, where it's clearer. Even though the water runs fast, which means it looks clear enough to drink without filtering, we always filter our water anyway.

I'm just about to slip my shoes off when I hear twigs crackling nearby.

"Pete, if you've tried to . . ."

I turn and freeze, dropping the filter bag, which falls onto the narrow bank and into the water. A grizzly bear cub is standing on its hind legs not even twenty feet downstream, staring at me and sniffing the air. Potentially the cutest thing on the planet, and not even all that scary. I would win that fight, easily, and just come away with some bad scratches. Not even a fight, really. It's the mama bear that is now a much bigger problem.

You're supposed to play dead if a grizzly comes at you, but Pete is up at the tent, so is the bear spray, and I don't know where the mama is, so there is no way that I'm staying put to wait for her, only to end up having to play dead, lying on my stomach with my arms protecting my head, as if an angry mama bear couldn't just punt me clear across the creek with one swipe, before or after she gouged my stomach out in one bite.

Don't wait.

Stand tall, say something, retrace your steps. Slowly.

But the "say something" is only if you want the bears to know that you're human, and that you're there, so they can watch you go away and get on with their foraging. This is a bear cub. And I don't want the mama bear to know that I'm here if she's far enough away not to hear me.

Which is a joke, Annie, I hear Pete's voice tell me, as if he's right beside me. *That bear can smell a carcass from twenty miles away.*

"But that's a carcass."

I'm not a carcass. Yet.

But what if she smells Pete?

Keep backing up the hill. Slow and steady.

I can't go slowly, though. What if the mama bear is up at the tent?

The cub wanders up to the rock with the water bladders and bottles on it. It swipes at them, and they all fall into the water. Less than a few seconds later, they've floated downstream and out of sight.

Don't think about that. Get to Pete.

To hell with it! I turn and sprint up to the top of the hill, my heart pounding so hard I can hardly see straight, but there is the bright orange tent, and no mama bear looking for the carcass of Pete's leg. That I can see. *Now* it's time to make noise.

"Hey, bear!" I holler. "We're little, tiny, terrified humans that you can kill with your giant, scary claws and your giant, scary teeth!"

Pete peers out of the tent.

"Bear cub! By the creek! I don't know where Mama is!" Loud and musical, to sound extra human. "Pot, pan, noise, now!" I sing.

He reaches for the pot, which is right there, still with oatmeal gunk in it, which is glaringly stupid, of course. He starts banging, and I start to relax just a little, because it's a horrible, obnoxious sound that would drive away pretty much anything with a heartbeat, deadly claws or not.

"Because what idiots do that in the backcountry?" I shout. "And now we have no water bottles and no water bladders because Baby Bear chucked them in the creek!" I holler to the warbling tune of absolutely nothing in particular.

"Really?" Pete yells in his bear singsong, which is much more pleasant than mine, even if it's at half power because he's so sick. "That is incredibly unfortunate, because drinking dirty water from our cooking pot is not ideal in the least! And if you go for help, you'll need to take it!"

"It stays with you!"

"You'll need it more than me!"

"No I won't!" I sing.

We both fall silent. Surely, that's enough to scare off the mama bear.

"I'm going to go look," I say.

Pete nods.

"I do have to go back down there to clean the pot and get more water." I take the pot. "Pass me the scrubber thingy?" He fishes in the little bag with all our cooking stuff in it and hands it to me.

"I can't believe you just asked for the scrubber thingy in the face of an impending grizzly attack."

"Scrubby thingies are essential in warding off a mama bear defending her postcard-cute baby bear." I laugh. "Didn't you know?"

"I do now," Pete says. "I do indeed."

From the edge of the slope, I can see exactly no bears, and no water vessels of any kind. I sprint down to the creek, take a few steps in, and scrub off the caked-on oatmeal as best as I can.

Once all the oatmeal gunk has been washed away, I fill the pot up to the top and secure the lid in place like we do when we pack it with the little folding stove and the fuel canister to hike to the next spot.

I owe Preet another apology.

The last time we saw a bear was just a couple of months ago, at the base of Ugly Mug. Pete and I had been climbing—me with ropes, him with no ropes—while Preet was setting out the picnic she had put together. Pete had offered to teach her how to climb, but she had zero interest. Instead, she was treating the day like it was a weird time-travel scene in a B movie.

"Are you seriously going to wear that?" I'd asked that morning when we picked her up. She was dressed in a crisp white dress that fell to her ankles and had a white satin sash tied in a bow at the back, like something the Jane Austen character in said time-travel movie would wear. White gloves with pearl buttons up to her elbows. A wide-brimmed straw hat decorated with flowers—fresh, not fake—and little black ankle boots with ribbon laces.

"Absolutely," she said as she lifted an enormous wicker picnic basket into the back of the truck. "You're lucky I'm not insisting we travel by horse and carriage."

"Don't deny her her Victorian picnic," Pete said from the driver's seat. "But you should keep the basket on your lap, Preet. It gets dusty on the way up."

So we drove half an hour with that basket half on her lap and half on mine.

Fine china plates, crystal glasses for the iced tea, silver knives and forks and spoons. Scones, thick cream, three different kinds of homemade jam in little jars with waxed cloth for lids. A loaf of bread she'd baked that morning, pasture-fed butter, pickled mango, tapenade, an entire watermelon—which is what made the basket so heavy—and five kinds of cheese.

There was more, but that's what she'd pulled out for us when we came down from our climb.

But that's not what we saw first.

What we saw first was Preet between the truck and the picnic spread, mostly obscured by a white parasol with tiny cherry blossoms on it, squatting down, arm outstretched, offering a large chunk of cheese to a bear cub. Scrawny and very little and probably just a couple of weeks out of the den, but a bear nonetheless.

"Stop!" Pete shouted.

"What the hell are you *doing*?" I yelled.

We ran to her, shouting and waving our hands, which sent the bear cub galloping into the woods.

When we got to her, she looked so out of place against the backdrop of the beat-up old truck and the Cascades behind her. And she clearly *was* in the wrong place and time if she was about to hand-feed a dangerous wild animal.

"That was pretty stupid, for a vegetarian," I said, not even trying to hold back my anger.

"It's just a baby," she said. "Is it really all that terrible to feed it? Did you see? How skinny it was?"

"*Because* it's a baby," Pete said. "It just came out of the den, Preet."

"A fed bear is a dead bear," I said. "What kind of idiot are you? Don't they tell you that at the airport when you get here?"

"Annie! That's a stupid thing to say." Pete took Preet's hand and headed for the picnic blanket. "And you know it."

"Actually," Preet said, "at the airport they say 'Welcome to

America,' if you're lucky. And if not, then good luck. Nothing about bears. Brown bears? No problem. Brown people?"

"I'm sorry," I said. "That was a dumb thing to say. Really dumb. Lots of stupid Americans feed bears too. Or chase bison at Yellowstone."

"I accept your apology." Preet kissed me on one cheek and then the other. "Now I won't feed anything. Not even those blue birds that beg."

"Steller's jays," Pete said. "But we feed those, so that's okay."

"Surely one nuisance animal is like the rest," Preet said. I could tell she was turning her wildlife lesson into a rule, which she would not go on to break. Which meant no more putting peanuts on our heads and waiting for a Steller's jay to swoop down and get them.

"You need to be afraid of bears," Pete said. "And be respectful of their space."

"Steller's jays are just fun."

The cooking pot is what the mama bear might've smelled from miles away. It's not feeding them Stilton by hand, but it's still mighty stupid. I'll happily tell that to Preet when we get home.

When Do You Know If It's Really That Bad?

I have never wished for a straw more than right now. Pete has to sit up every time he wants a drink, and every time I think he should have a drink, no matter how much he protests. Water is all we have for medicine, so to speak. I've pillaged our packs, looking for something better to use as a cup, but we only have our bowls, which are also our mugs and too shallow.

We empty one pot. Then two. And the whole while neither of us talks about me leaving to get help. Things feel calm, like maybe he's improving. I just want to wait, until morning, and then see.

Pete pees into a plastic bag, which I empty and rinse and give back to him. We don't talk about that either. Especially not about how dark his pee is, like cloudy apple cider.

✧ ✧ ✧

We both fall asleep, but for how long, I don't know. When I wake up, it's dusk. I watch Pete sleep, the blue twilight making the shadows long. I can still see the sweat dripping off his face. The very tips of his ears and nose are almost black. His chest rises with quick, shallow breaths, and I am thankful for each one.

It is time to go.

While he sleeps, I empty my pack of anything he might need while I'm gone. I lift his head to slide off his lanyard with his whistle on it. I put the first-aid kit by his head, even though there isn't much in there now. I take out my extra layer and fold it and my quick-dry towel and set them with the first-aid kit. I leave him the last two energy bars and PowerGels, which are pretty much all the food we have left, except for oatmeal and two packets of miso soup. I don't know why we have so little, but it will have to do. I take one bar and one gel. I'm not going to be gone that long.

I empty the one dry bag we have for our electronics and take it and the pot to the creek and fill both. On the way back, I stop to build a big "SOS" with rocks. Even if it's easy to see from here, it will be harder from the sky. I glance up. The smoke cover is like a wide, foul bank of clouds. Which will need to part for the rescue helicopter.

Pete is awake, trying to sit up. He knocks the pot over, and my heart sinks. I fill it from the wet bag and set it outside on the stove to boil so I can make him miso soup.

"You have to watch out for the pot," I say as I help him up to drink the soup once it's ready. "That's the one thing you cannot knock over. So this was your pass. I'm going to fill it again, but you're not going to knock it over again. Spill your pee bag, but not the pot."

"I don't know what you're talking about," he says with a weak grin. "I don't pee in a bag. That's for people with tubes up their dicks."

"Of course. You don't pee in a bag. Which is why I haven't managed to find you two more to not pee in. Do yourself a favor, okay? Try to do up the bags that you're not peeing into."

"Got it."

He leans against me, heavy and so hot. His shirt is soaked with sweat. "Please, Pete. Please, please, please let me try the stretcher. Come with me." My cheek against his back as I cry.

I need him.

I *need* him.

"You know what I was thinking?" Forget about the stretcher. There is no time. It won't work because we are not even on a real *trail*. "I owe Preet an apology about that bear she was trying to feed. Because how many times did we hang up our food this trip?"

"None."

"Right. We're the idiots, I'll tell her so. Okay?"

He nods, his eyes squeezed shut. "Tell her I'm sorry."

"Tell her yourself."

"You tell her."

"You tell her! Don't be an ass, Pete! If you have something

to say to her, then you can tell her yourself. That guy didn't die! That guy *didn't die.*"

Please, God.

If you let him live, I will believe in you.

"You have the compass," he says. "You have the map, if it can help. Get to the PNT and you'll find someone. Even if you never find the trail, you'll hit the big river, you'll find a road. There has to be someone. Loggers, cattlemen, homesteaders. Fishermen. Hunters."

"It's June, Pete."

"No it's not." He shakes his head. "It's September. Otis Creek." He opens the tin of talismans. He picks out a perfect cube of pyrite. "You found this today. Otis Creek."

"We're not that close to home." I lift out the crystal. "We found this a few days ago. We met Ty and Paola."

"I like them. We should go to their shop." He remembers that detail, that they have a tiny rock and gem shop in Sedro-Woolley. That's good. "I know where we are, Annie. Who is the better navigator?"

"Neither of us," I say. "Because here we are."

Otis Creek, and home, is hundreds of miles from here. That much I know for sure. I wish we were there too, because then I would know exactly how to get help.

Later, when the moon is rising and I have werewolves on my mind, he has a seizure and spills my talismans all over the dirt and then kicks them out into the great who-knows-where of the very nearby woods. When I pull him back into the tent, I glance away into the dark where the talismans went, but instead of any familiar glint, there is the orange glow of flames simmering lower on the ridge. Heading toward us.

Never mind the talismans. They don't matter now. I try to make my voice light, and I think I do a pretty good job of it as I listen to myself make words come out of my mouth.

"I will permit one more seizure," I say. "Got it, Mr. Unicorn Pete Alvarez Bonner? But you are *not* allowed to die here."

His lips are dry again, so I find his lip balm in his pocket and put some on. Unicorn Poo lip balm, sparkly, vanilla-sweet.

"Have some water, and then we'll make a plan."

There are only two possible plans. I stay, or I go.

"This is not the way that you die, Pete." The water dripping off the towel is warm. He's not opening his mouth, but I manage to get enough in that he swallows. Or tries to swallow. He ends up coughing, and his already flushed face turns nearly purple. "We're alive today, right? Just think of all the times that you didn't die. That *we* didn't die. We can put this in our Notebook of Doom as soon as we get home."

Stay, Annie. Go. Stay. Go. What would Pete do? For a long while after the seizure, he's just mumbling and stretching and chewing the air like it's a big raw carrot, then he slowly becomes more alert, which surprises me.

"Do you know where we are, Pete?"

"Lost, mostly."

"But where?"

"South of the PNT. The fire is close," he says. "To the east."

West.

"Too close."

Stay with him, Annie.

We've used the last of the antibiotics; all we have left is Tylenol. I put two in his hand and then tip the pot of water to his lips. He swallows with a cough.

"Go," he says. "Why should two of us get engulfed?"

"Because we stick together."

"That's stupid." Pete shakes his head. "Besides, Gigi and your dad would kill me."

Does he think Gigi is still alive?

"*Go,* Annie." He takes my hand. His is clammy and cold, the tips of his fingers gray. "If you stay, it'll be like I killed you."

"No one is getting killed."

"Go," he says. "While you're gone, I'll try to find your talismans."

I tip the pot to his lips and help him drink.

"I found them all." Not even one. "When you were sleeping. Besides, you seem a bit better right now."

"I'm glad that you found them." He struggles to finish the water, but he does. I run down to the creek one last time, coming back with a full pot.

"I won't knock it over," he laughs. "And I won't get confused and pee in it. I won't drink my pee, even if it's the last thing I do."

"You're not going to die." I sit behind him, my legs on either side. I hug him, but he winces, so I just put my cheek to his sweaty back. "We've almost died before, and we never did. Right?"

"This is different."

"You'll turn a corner."

"And die."

"Pete! Stop saying that!" But he is so hot and sweaty that I can't imagine him being well anytime, and his wound is oozing pus, with bright red streaks like a starburst all around.

He's fallen asleep again. I tuck him into his bag, with the top wide open because it's still warm. I write him a note and leave it on the pot.

Dear Pete. I'll be back with help and a big iced tea and a bag of barbecue chips. Drink water. Eat if you can. I love you, my person.
PS. Please, please, please be careful with the water.

I'm ready to go.

"See you later, Unicorn Pete. I love you."

I follow his arm to his wrist. Strong radial pulse. Blood pressure is still okay. I remember the wilderness first-aid instructor telling us to always check the pulse at the wrist first, because if that's gone, but there's a strong pulse at the neck, the person is starting to circle the drain.

"You're good, Pete." I kiss him on the cheek. "I should be

back by morning. With help! You're okay. You're going to be okay." I kiss him on the other cheek, and then his forehead, and his lips too. I pull away suddenly. Every part of him is hot, but not his lips. They are cold. As cold as my hands, and as pale.

This is not happening.

None of this is really happening, which is why it's going to be easy.

We used to say that to each other if we got scared.

This isn't really happening. Something else is. We just don't know what yet.

Out of the tent, with my pack strapped on my back, I'm struck by two thoughts at the same time.

The smoke is even thicker than it was hours ago.

And what about the bear?

Ignore the thoughts, Annie. I check the compass and head north. As fast as I can with the forest floor tripping me up.

Don't think about the fire. Don't think about the bear.

We saw wolves once, in the distance. I've lost count of how many black bear encounters we've had. A cougar tracked us all the way to the top of a mountain once, and Pete's dad shot it. We've seen a badger, a porcupine, a lynx, a bobcat, and different kinds of raptors. Even the tail end of a rattlesnake slithering away between two sun-hot rocks above Ellensburg when we were looking for blue agates and I found an arrowhead instead.

But I have never seen a grizzly before today. Even if it was a cub.

Will it come for Pete?

Can it smell that he's weak?

Or what if the grizzly follows *me*?

Annie, Annie, Annie, Annie, shut up and keep going. Just *go.*

The trees thin, so now I can run, my headlamp bouncing as I jump over logs and rocks, heading steadily north.

It's harder to see because of all the smoke, but the small circle of light I do have is enough. Once I find the trail, I will run faster, even though my lungs are already burning. Last year the newspaper said the smoke was so bad that it was like everyone was smoking eleven cigarettes a day, even babies. This smoke is even worse.

North to the Pacific Northwest Trail, where there will be someone to help. I am sure of it.

My lungs feel like they're being scorched from the inside out. I can't catch a full breath, and so after a while—who knows how long—I get dizzy, and then all of a sudden I trip on a root and go down hard, my head knocking a mossy log, a hot, searing pain filling my head, pushing behind my eyes. I am flat on my back, panting, as the forest spins around me. My head pounds. There's a terrible ringing in my ears. Everything is foggy, like the smoke is right in my face, even though I know it's not. I reach up and feel damp on my temple. My fingers come away with blood. A lot of it.

This is stupid.

I should've never left him.

I don't know where I am.

I don't know where the trail is.

I won't know where *he* is, pretty soon.

Before I lose him, I have to try to take him with me. That way, whatever happens, we'll be together. He's rested for, what, over a day now? This is the most energy he'll have.

Don't kid yourself, Annie. He's not going anywhere.

Okay, then. Okay. Okay . . .

Then I'll bring help to *him*.

I'll set a fire on the other side of the creek, and someone on the PNT will report it, and then a fire crew will come, and *that* is how we will go together.

By doing the worst thing, I will save the best thing.

The ringing in my ears is so loud now, it sounds like a machine is making the noise somewhere nearby in the forest.

My heartbeat has slowed, but now each pulse ricochets in my head like a gunshot, and my lungs refuse to fill with any more smoke, no matter how hard I try to control my breathing, catch enough breath to keep going. I need to keep going. I roll onto my knees to push myself up, but as soon as I'm on two feet, I tip over, and everything goes black.

⟡ ⟡ ⟡

When I come to, my lungs still hurt, but I'm not as dizzy. If I've ever needed something to play out with a Hollywood ending, this is it. And it's not happening. I reverse my bearing and head south, back to Pete. I walk fast, but I don't run. I cannot afford to pass out again. I am unraveling, but even as I do, I can't let myself fall apart until I fix this.

Turning Back

When I think about Pete, I cannot breathe in. When I question whether I should've left him, I can't breathe out. I try not to think about it, or else I get dizzy with not being able to breathe, and my head gets light and the air in front of me sparkles and I feel like I'll fall. I can't think about the wildfires either, because that makes me think of Pete. I can't think about the grizzly, because that makes me think of Pete.

The truth is that every single thought comes back to Pete.

This is as close as I've ever been to dying. And Pete is even closer than me. If I don't find him help and get him out of here, this will be the end.

There is only one other time when I really thought we would die. We make fun of the other times, in our Notebook of Doom. But there is a story that we haven't written in there yet, because it's too dark to share the pages.

⟡ ⟡ ⟡

It was a brown car. Long and low. Not a gangster car. It was clean but pretty beat-up.

"Rust along the bottom of the doors." I tell the story to the forest, to keep the bears and the cougars and wildfire away. "A cautionary tale!" I shout. "Don't get into cars with strangers, kids!" I keep talking to myself. "Who does that? We knew better." I tell the story to Pete too, even though he's heard it a thousand times. He's the only one, though. Not another soul knows what happened that day.

Except Mel.

Pete said, "Your mom hitchhiked all the time when she was younger." Pete said that if she did it, then it wasn't all that stupid, right? Pete said she'd hitchhiked all around America and Europe. Pete said, "No problem, Annie. Besides, how else can we get there? It's not like we're going to be a couple of kids standing on the highway with our thumbs out."

And I wasn't going to be the kid who mentioned that even though my mom did all those brave, exciting things, she still did the most cowardly thing of all.

So I just agreed, and we asked people at the gas station neither of our fathers ever went to instead.

"Excuse me, ma'am, we got the bus here to visit our grandpa, and now we need a ride back to Diablo Lake."

Where my mom had been living, in a cabin just before the ecology center, where she'd been a cleaning lady, which was news to us until the police came to our door. We were going to find the cabin and see her things before my dad and Gigi went up the next day to clear it out.

The man who said yes told us to both ride in the back because it was safer. There was a Christian talk radio station on low, and even though he doesn't believe in God, Pete said that meant he was a good man. My mom had never had any trouble, Pete said.

Never any trouble, I thought. Never any trouble.

"Melford Osmond," he said. "Call me Mel."

"Ron and Hermione," I said.

Pete punched my arm.

Why I thought to give him the wrong names, I'm not sure. Likely, my twelve-year-old intuition, which should've given us a hint that something wasn't quite right.

He stopped at the general store in Newhalem and let us out.

"Go ahead and pick a treat, Ron and Hermione."

We each picked a Drumstick from the freezer, and the woman at the till said, "What nice kids," and Mel put his hand on Pete's head.

"I couldn't ask for better grandkids," Mel said. That's when we knew, because our little name lie and his big lie added up to Pete and me sharing a look that said, *What the heck are we going to do?* He had a hand on each of our shoulders, and his fingers were digging in. "Get in the car, kids!" All happy, and waving to the woman inside as he got in and locked the doors.

When he drove off the highway onto a dirt road, we didn't

say anything, just held hands and watched the trees speeding by as our ice cream melted on the floor of the car.

"All the other times weren't close, but that's the day you almost died, Pete!" I scream it at the forest. "You and me both! For real!"

The other times are funny.

But that man who left finger marks on our shoulders, he was the devil who almost took us. He was the real boogeyman, because what other kind of monster would dare to come for a child just days after she lost her mother?

We came to a bridge over a deep, slow river, its surface so glassy and calm it looked like a lake. Just past that, a yellow gate across the road. When Mel stopped to unlock it, we didn't even have to consult each other before we got out and ran back to the bridge and jumped off.

He was shouting, but he stayed up there on the bridge. He didn't even get back into the car and try to track us along the road. He just shouted about how he was only going to show us a really amazing thing.

We held hands and floated on our backs, and I didn't think of my mother for the rest of the day, which was the very definition of a miracle.

It was a hot day.

The water was deliciously cold, especially for two alive kids.

The sun burned our faces so bad that Pete's dad put aloe

vera all over, like a beauty mask. He had no idea that we'd even run away. We said we'd lost our backpacks in the bush when we went to pick mushrooms. Another lemonade stand to pay to replace them before school started. We were such happy kids after the bruises on our shoulders faded.

Such happy kids, for a while.

"Not today!" I screamed, the tall trees like silent sentinels all around. "You are not dying today, Pete Alvarez Bonner!"

Finding Pete

It must be another hour or more before the black, smoky night sky slowly eases into pinks and purples. Birds start singing.

Finally, I see it. The bright orange of our little tent, the even brighter reflective tape we patched the side with last year after I snagged it on blackberry bushes when I was taking it down.

I run faster.

"Pete!" I'm leaping over logs and dodging big rocks like some kind of superhero. If only I'd been so agile and fast last night, I might've gotten to the trail. "Pete! I'm coming!"

I open the vestibule and crawl in. His back is to me. He's taken his shirt off. His shoulders glisten with sweat.

"Pete?"

No answer. A few seconds pass, and then I hear him. "Drink some water. I bet you didn't have any, did you?"

"No." I pull the bag out, and it's empty; the whole bottom

of my backpack is soaked. "I'll have some of yours and replace it. Please tell me you didn't pee in it."

Right this minute, though, I just want to lie down and rest. Just for a second, and then we'll figure it out. "I have a plan," I say. I don't, but I need to say it. I am hoping that I will have a plan very, very soon.

"A plan is good, Annie."

I kick off my shoes, already getting chilled because of being soaked with sweat. I slide into my sleeping bag and spoon him.

"I passed out," I tell him. "After I fell and hit my head on a log. You would've laughed."

Not a sound.

I scramble out of my bag and pull him over to the middle of the tent.

His mouth is open, his head tipped back just a bit. His earlobes are turning black, and the tip of his nose. His chest is rising with short, shallow breaths. One eye is open. The other one is half shut. He smells sour.

"Oh, Pete." This was too fast. I don't understand! It was just a cut! How did it go from just the stick on the cliff to this? It makes no sense.

He didn't tell me to drink some water. He didn't say anything. That was in my head. I reach for his hand. It's even colder than mine. No radial pulse. I fall over him to check his other wrist. Nothing.

I put my fingers to his throat. There's his pulse. Strong, rapid. Too fast.

"Pete." I unzip my sleeping bag. "You have to stay alive. You have to. I'll follow the creek, you know? There's always something by the water eventually, right? I'll look at the maps again. Maybe we missed something." I unzip his bag. He's peed himself. Long enough ago that it's dried up now. His leg is mottled purple below the knee.

I quickly zip the bag back up.

It's the strangest sensation. I'm crying, but there are no tears, because I can't even remember the last time I drank any water. My muscles burn with pain, but I just want to run. I am terrified, but there is no panic. I am devastatingly sad, but I know I can fix this. I am tired, but I cannot sleep.

So I talk.

I get everything ready for him. Water in the bags. His headlamp within reach. I tell him that the only reason we are friends is because Ms. Hayward paired him up with me for reading time.

I hear a tiny chuckle.

"Remember that?" I bend down and touch his hot shoulder. "She called you a reluctant reader. And I was already reading *Voyage of the Dawn Treader.* She thought I could fix you."

"Fix me." Pete smiles.

"I will," I say. "I'm just about ready to go."

When I run out of things to say, I start singing "Down in the Valley," which Gigi taught us. "You should have a nice song to sing to me when I'm in the old folks' home," she'd say. "No Tom Jones." She never made it to the old folks' home, but Pete and I know all the words anyway. We sang it when we heard bears huffing just off the trail. Or when we had a campfire and we ran out of the cheesy "Quartermaster's Store" verses. We never sang "Kumbaya." Not even when we were at summer camp and all the other kids were singing it and the camp counselors scowled at us over their guitar.

Down in the valley, the valley so low,
Hang your head over, hear the wind blow.
Hear the wind blow, dear, hear the wind blow.
Hang your head over, hear the wind blow.
Roses love sunshine, violets love dew.
Angels in heaven know—

We sang that to Gigi. A lot. In the two weeks it took her to go from not-talking to dead. She died of dehydration, really. If we'd had her in a hospital, on a feeding tube, she might've lived for weeks longer.

But when you're dying, why take the long way around?

I know what's happening.

In the minutes before Gigi's heart actually stopped, something shifted in the air. It was as if the air had sweetened, and thinned, making a gossamer veil between this world of the living and the place of the not-living, whatever that is. The air in the tent is thin now too. And while it doesn't smell sweet, like it did when Gigi died, I can't smell the decay and filth I know is all around me.

"It's okay to go."

And then she did. Her mouth open, gawping to catch three

more breaths, so spread out that I wondered with each one if it was her last. I lay alongside her, just like this. Holding on to her, just like this. Taking her through the veil, just like this.

There was no one to hold my mother's hand when she died.

But maybe her death was quicker. No lingering, like with Gigi.

And Pete.

Because Pete is dying.

"I'm ready to go. I won't be gone long," I say. "I love you, Pete."

He says it back. I know it. I can't hear it, but his lips move, and I can feel the slightest puff of air on my cheek as I lean in close. Those are his last words. *I love you, Annie.* There is nothing anyone can say about the process of dying and physiological impossibilities that will make me believe otherwise, because I am kneeling beside my most important person in all the world, and he isn't breathing anymore.

JUNE 27

Pete's cheeks look hollow, and all along the bottom of him, his blood is pooling, which happened with Gigi. Lividity.

We laughed about Gigi. She would have been livid about looking so gross after she died. I touch his pale cheeks. All the shocking red has drained. He is beyond cold.

This happened with Gigi too. At some point, the body becomes just that. A body. Any part of who that person was is gone. But he still looks like himself. Sort of. He looks like he's ready to do the zombie walk at Halloween.

I can't think of his body as Pete anymore.

Not if I'm going to leave him. If I think of him as Pete, then I'll just stay with him until I die too, because no one is going to find us. We are absolutely unfindable.

⬦ ⬦ ⬦

I slide my hand into one of his pockets and pull out his knife and the truck keys, and in the other I find a bunch of pieces of folded paper.

I pull them out, several at a time, and recognize what they are at once. Origami unicorn heads. At least two dozen of them.

Each one has a name printed on it in tiny block letters that are almost impossible to read. But I can. Preet, Preet, his dad. His dead mom, my dead mom, dead Gigi, his dad. My dad, Preet, Preet. None with my name on it, and instead of feeling left out, I feel relief. I don't want a last-thing-I-have-to-tell-you-before-I-die message from him. If there were one with my name, I would burn it. With that thought, I consider doing the same with the ones in my hands. Maybe no one should see these? Won't it make everyone's heart hurt more? Except for the dead mothers, that is.

I let them fall to the tent floor. Which is when I see a small book open facedown near his pack, and his favorite pen. I pick up the pen first and let the tiny unicorn slide through the glitter one way and then the other, before I reach to pick up the book just to see what he was reading without me.

As my fingers light upon it, I realize with a shotgun jolt to my heart exactly what it is.

The diary that my mother tried to give me that night. The one with the unicorn on the front. The one I shoved under the seat and never thought about again.

I pulled my mother's letter out of the diary in his pack that night by the hemlocks. That's what the book was.

I let my fingers rest on it while my mind tries to sort out what's happening. I am in a tiny, hot tent with wildfires all around, and my best friend is dead, and now here is the thing that I would least expect to come across. I would be less surprised if I saw a real live unicorn down at the creek having a drink, with a rainbow arching overhead. I don't understand, but at the same time, I know exactly what's happened, because there is only one answer. He took it from the car that night, or maybe after, but that's what he did. And the letter was in it.

Pete has had it this whole time.

"Pete." I look at him, which is the most natural thing for me to do. "Why did you take this?" I drop my eyes back to the book. I've looked at Pete ten million times since we were little kids, but now I know why you can't look at dead people the same way you look at them when they're alive, even if you still love them as much. It's still Pete, but it's not Pete too. There is a subtraction of something, and an addition of something, and now it just does not compute. "This wasn't yours to take, Pete."

But then, what did I think happened to it? Truthfully, I completely forgot about it, considering what happened a few days later, but I might've guessed that my dad found it and threw it out because it would've hurt me too much to have it—probably true—or that Gigi put it up in a closet somewhere for me to have when I got older, like how she gave me my mom's jewelry along with hers just before she died, none of which I've looked at or worn because it does hurt too much. But I never would've guessed that twelve-year-old Pete took it from the car and kept it from me for all these years, along with the letter.

It's open about halfway through to a spread full of his small, slanty writing, the pages warped with dampness.

Dear Annie,
  If you are reading this—

My stomach churns, and for a moment I think I might throw up. Instead, I slam the diary shut and stuff it into my pack, along with his knife, all the paper unicorns, and the last protein bar.

I drag Pete and the tent out from under the tree so it will be easy to spot from overhead, because I'm coming back for him, as soon as I can, and it will probably be in a plane.

"You won't even miss me," I say as I take out the poles. The airy material relaxes slowly down, covering him in a shroud of bright orange. I thought it was a good idea, but as soon as I see it flattened over him, I see his shape too. His brow, his nose, chin, chest, his giant feet.

I collapse down onto my knees and cry some more, but again, no tears. I need water. I'm almost out of food.

Pete would be yelling at me by now.

Go! Go, Annie!

✧ ✧ ✧

I know that being in the direct sun will make him decompose faster, but whenever I let that thought in, I stop in my tracks and am immobile for an achingly long time. I can't think about the word "decompose." But I do, and then I think about how it doesn't matter, really, because he wants to be cremated.

"Burn or bury?" he asked me once when we were sleeping out at Otis Creek. It was a hot midsummer night last year, before Preet. We were just lying on top of our sleeping bags, staring at the stars, wide awake almost all night, talking about everything. If you'd tracked our subjects and marked each one with a pin of light, it would've made a tangle of a constellation.

"Bury," I said. "But just under a tree somewhere. Not in a box. Not embalmed or anything. Just me, in some dirt. There are graveyards that will let you do that."

"You just want to rot?"

"Kinda. Yeah. Genuine worm food. You?"

"Burn. Definitely."

"What about your ashes?"

"Haven't thought that far."

Yet here we are now, the flames on the ridge likely moving closer, even if they look like they are standing still, just a wavering line of fierce heat warping the sky.

Stay there, wildfire.

Just *stay.*

✧ ✧ ✧

There is no way this is going to be easy, so I just do up the clasps on my pack, turn on my heel, and start running.

"Back in a bit, Pete!" I run due east, along the creek. I'm going to follow the water. That's something they teach you about being lost in the wilderness. Staying put is the best advice. But if you can't stay put, follow the water. Water almost always leads to people.

"Love you!" I call over my shoulder. "Love you," I whisper as I run. Over logs, through prickly bushes that scratch my arms and legs. "I love you." I run as if I have all the energy in the world. As if I ate a giant plate of pasta the night before. As if there is no smoke. As if I've been well hydrated for days. I run so fast that, almost four hours later, I come upon the Pacific Northwest Trail.

"Yes!" I look around. Not a soul for as far as I can see. Which makes sense, because who the hell would be hiking in the middle of wildfires?

I keep running. East. The word pounding with my heart. *East, east, east.*

The sun slants. I know the day is heading for sunset. But I have my headlamp, and so I can keep going.

Then I see it, a glint off to the northeast.

A truck on a road?

I squint. No. A roof! Not even five hundred yards away, off the trail to the south; I scan the land between here and there. It's on the other side of the creek. It looks pretty lazy from up here. Totally crossable. I make a beeline for it. If it's abandoned and there is no clearly better trail, I'll just come back up to the PNT. I have to try. It's the only sign of civilization I've seen since we met the people who were digging for crystals.

I sprint down the shale, slipping and sliding and falling, until I get to the bottom of the slope. I can still see the roof, but the sun is starting to set. The light is filtered now, all the blues of the day blurring together.

When I get to the creek, I put my pack on my head and wade right in. Everything in my pack is in a big, thick plastic bag, so as long as I can keep hold of it, it doesn't matter if it gets wet.

I move at an angle and against the current, like the SAS book says. The water is up to my armpits, but my feet stay on the ground. In the middle of the creek, I stop and think about how nice it would be to just lean back and let go. Let my pack fill up with water and disappear to the silty bottom while I float downstream, on my back, staring up at the sky and imagining all the stars that are hiding behind the smoke.

There is no rush.

I won't be able to find him again.

If the fire keeps heading toward him, it will cremate him, and the wind will spread his ashes better than I ever could. I let my pack drop, still holding it with one hand.

No one needs to open those unicorns.

I don't need to read what he wrote to me, or what else that diary is filled with.

We could all just drift down the river, like that time Pete and I did, holding hands and getting so cold, so fast.

I lean back, about to let go, but then I hear barking. Very, very close. I open my eyes and see two big dogs on the shore.

"What the hell you doing, girl?" An old man scrambles down to the water's edge. The dogs whine as he wades in and grabs me and pulls me to the shore, where I notice he's got two—now wet—dead rabbits tied to his belt. "An idiot's baptism or something? Thought I was going to watch you float away, for Pete's sake. Likely no coming back from that."

For *Pete's* sake.

The deer.

The other deer.

"Come with me," the man says. "Need to get you dried up and warmed up. No arguments. I'm no creep in the woods. I got kids and grandkids and I'd do the same for any of them." As if to prove that he isn't a bad man, he takes out his wallet and shows me pictures of several blond children, and two with hair and skin so brown that their brightly colored clothes nearly glow on them.

He sees my face.

"Oh, don't worry." He takes out one of the photos. "I got them laminated at that print shop in town. Waterproof. Hell of a thing." One of the dogs—more of a puppy—bounces around me, sniffing my shoes, nudging me from one side and then the other.

"Yellow-headed ones are my daughter's kids. Twins and a little one," he says as he leads me up the bank to a short trail.

"The little one is a doll. Just precious. Those twins, though. Run for your money. They do good up here when I put them to work."

I have everything to say to him, but I can't make myself say any of it, so I let him talk, which he is obviously happy to do.

"The other two are my son's boys," he says. "He married a woman from Ghana. They've got another on the way, although I'm thinking it might be twins. Runs in my family. I'm a twin. Mine are twins. Handfuls, twins."

The younger dog jumps up and licks my face, while the old one looks away, like he is embarrassed. He's barely moved from where he's been sitting, waiting for some kind of direction.

"The good old dog there is Mister." The old man gives him a pat, and the dog falls in beside me as we start to walk. "The other one I don't know yet. As for me, you can call me Shook. Most people do. Like the Elvis song. Used to do a great impression of the King. Name stuck."

Tell him about Pete.

No. Not yet.

Why not?

The simple answer is because then it would be too real. Because I don't even want them to find him. Maybe I want the fire to take him. He would like that. I know. And maybe all of these thoughts confuse me, and I'm not sure of anything except the next step I take, and only after I've taken it.

I glance up the mountain behind me. There is so much less smoke down here that I can imagine the wildfire isn't that bad. I can breathe more easily. The campfire smell is fainter, enough that I can also smell the pine trees and salal bushes warmed by the sun—which is still bright orange down here too—and the old man himself, who smells like greasy body odor and Irish Spring soap, which is a smell I know only because my dad hangs it in the garden to keep the deer out.

Shook leads me to a very old but very tidy shack, where the first thing I notice is about three dozen chickens pecking at the patchy grass around a broken-down rust-bucket truck up on blocks, a quad, a tangle of bikes, and a well-maintained driveway that no doubt leads to the road that takes him into town, where the print shop—and the rest of civilization—is.

"I'll make you a cup of coffee," he says. "Or you want some hot chocolate instead?"

I can't imagine drinking either, considering the nausea in my gut that threatens to explode out both ends. But I know I need the strength.

"Hot chocolate, please." I rest my hand on the younger dog's big, blocky head while Shook goes ahead into the cabin. "You need a name, dog." I squat, and he hooks a great big paw on my shoulder, nearly tipping me over. "I'm going to call you Otis. For the creek."

He wags his tail.

"You're a good dog, Otis." His tail thumps the ground,

sending a cloud of dirt up, which attracts several chickens for some reason. They cluck and grumble at my feet. I put a hand out, and a couple of the chickens come closer, two of the littlest ones, both with green-black feathers and shiny red combs.

Otis doesn't like me taking my attention off of him, so he butts me with his big head. I give him a hug, and he leans into me with so much force that I end up sitting on my ass in the dirt, which startles the chickens and sends them scattering. When he finally lets me get up, he's wagging his tail so hard that it feels like a whip against my legs.

"Hungry?" Shook shouts from inside the cabin. "Want something to eat?"

Reluctantly, I follow Otis into the cabin so I can answer without shouting back. There is not one single shout in me. There are hardly any words either, because if I really start talking, I'll tell him all about Pete, and I'm not ready for that. I don't see a ham radio. Or a phone. Or even a walkie-talkie.

"Yes, sir. Thank you. Do you have a phone?"

"I do not," he says. "There's a radio in the shed. But it's in about ten pieces and absolutely useless. I can take you to the gas station. There's a pay phone there."

"That's okay," I say. "I don't need it right now."

"Good thing you found your way off the mountain," he says as he hands me a stack of clothes. "They came around with the evacuation notice, but I'm not going this time. The hell with it. I'll be like that old man who didn't leave when Mount St. Helens blew. Worse ways to go."

I see Pete, flushed red, his toes and lips turning black. Such a worse way. I squeeze my eyes shut, pushing the image back just far enough not to talk about it. Don't talk about it. Let the fire take him.

"Live here year-round now my better half's gone," Shook says. "My kids think I'm nuts, but I'd rather die out here in a wildfire than in an old folks' home."

Now I'm thinking of Gigi. She always said she'd put herself on an ice floe if we ever tried to get her into a home. She said we could sing "Down in the Valley" as she drifted away, but no way was a stranger going to change her diaper and be in control of what was on the TV.

"Those'll be big. But dry. Change in there." He points to the only other room.

"Come on, Otis," I say, and then catch myself. "I just called him that. I know it's not his name or anything. Sorry."

"I don't mind a bit." Shook shrugs. "Otis it is. I'll wring your clothes out and hang them up if you want. They'll dry a lot faster that way."

"Yes, please. Thank you."

Otis, newly christened, follows me in, sitting politely when I close the door behind him.

⟡ ⟡ ⟡

I peel everything off until I'm naked. Otis stands at the foot of the single bed. This is the old man's room. A grandfather clock in the corner takes up most of the space. A wristwatch and some change on a small bureau under the window, which hasn't been cleaned in forever. Prints of pen-and-ink geese tacked to the wall. I wonder if his wife drew those. One of his kids? Or maybe he did. Otis jumps up onto the bed, his mouth hanging open in a smile, drooling. He is truly a mutt. I have no idea what kind of dog he is, or what mix he is. Big. A bunch of kinds of gray. White muzzle. Lanky.

"Get off the bed, Otis Creek."

And as if he knows his name, he does.

I pull on Shook's shirt and a pair of shorts that won't stay up.

Shook gives me a piece of rope for a belt and goes outside with my clothes and puts them through an actual wringer machine. He hangs them on the clothesline and then heads back inside to light a camp stove that obviously has a permanent spot on the counter, even though everyone knows it's dangerous to use propane indoors. He skins and guts the rabbits in less than a minute each and then adds the meat to a pan with onions and garlic. He takes half a dozen dirty eggs from a big wire basket sitting at the other end of the counter. He gives them a quick rinse and cracks them and scrambles them up with some powdered milk and spinach and cheese.

I eat and he talks, eating while he does, the eggs all green and slimy as he chews and goes on about his kids and the cabin and the river being so low this year. The eggs and the rabbit are the best things I have ever eaten in my life, without an ounce of exaggeration. I can practically feel the protein working into my exhausted muscles, knitting them back into the shape they'll need to be when I leave here.

After it's dark out, he makes up the sagging, greasy old couch.

"I'd put you in the loft, but nothing's made up yet," he says. "Grandkids were going to be coming next week, but now with the fire, who knows when."

"I'm not sure how long I'll stay," I say.

"Until morning, when I'll drive you into town."

Morning seems so far away, though. I don't think I can wait that long, even if I really, really want to.

"I know bone-tired when I see it," he says. "We'll go first thing."

Otis hops up onto the couch beside me as I lie down and curl on my side. He nearly shoves me off as he circles and circles behind my knees before finally getting comfortable and settling down.

Shook and his old dog retire to the little bedroom. When he shuts the door, I find my headlamp and dig in my pack for the diary.

It is so much smaller than I remember. Not much bigger than a paperback. I remember that it had a lock, but there isn't one now. The corners are worn down to the cardboard underneath the shiny cover. The stars still sparkle. The unicorn is still trying to make that leap over the moon, which is still full and shimmering.

Why did you take it, Pete?

I open it, fully expecting to see my mother's handwriting. My hands start shaking, my breath quickens. A thumping white noise gets louder and louder in my head. I can hardly believe that I can feel even less steady than I already do.

Other than those two pages Pete filled, the rest of it is blank. I flip back to the front. Now I'm mad. Why didn't she fill it for me? Why didn't she fill every page, back and front, with things she wanted to say to me?

I find the pages Pete wrote on, but I don't read them.

If I read what he wrote, I'll be reading a message from dead Pete.

I'm not ready for that.

When I was little, I thought the worst day of my life was the day my dad left. And then I thought it was the day they found my mom's body. When Gigi died, that trumped both of those days. Now this day is the worst, and nothing will ever be worse. It is ten minutes away from midnight, when this day will officially be over and the next day will begin. I don't know what tomorrow will be like. The sun will come up, but the dark of it will be just as bad as the last dark moments of today.

I have to rest. Just long enough to gather the energy to get moving again. I shove the diary deep down into my pack and curl back up on the couch and close my eyes, even though I am sure that I will never, ever sleep again. Not while Pete is up on the mountain with fire closing in from two directions. I will rest an hour or so and then go. Otis sets his big head on my thigh and whines, as if he knows more about my plans than I do and doesn't like them.

Day Nine

JUNE 28

I wake up with a start in the middle of the night, right out of a dream where Pete is dead in the tent with rosy cheeks and his glitter lip balm and the unicorn diary in his crossed arms, like he was arranged like that for his own funeral, except when I look out of the tent, the flames are right there. Where the hell am I? I scramble out from under—what? What is that? A dog? Where's Pete? I'm in some kind of cabin. It smells dank. As my eyes adjust to the dark, I see the propane stove on the counter, the quilt, the shirt that I'm wearing—

Where is Pete?

What the hell am I wearing?

The dog butts me with his big, blocky head and whines.

Otis.

"I remember *you,*" I whisper, patting his head. He butts me again.

Then I remember, not in pieces, but all at once, like I missed a catch in dodgeball and took it in the gut instead. I bend over, hit hard, breathless.

Pete is up there on the mountain, in that tent, the wildfire closing in.

"I'm okay with that," I say to myself. "I am. I am."

I picture the flames, willowy orange and hot, licking toward our tent. Calm, peaceful, quick.

But I can't imagine calm or peaceful or quick. I just imagine terrible cracking and snapping and crashing as the pine trees roast and topple, the animals fleeing with terrified eyes, the awful roar like a million angry beasts of hell, rocks snapping in half.

No. Absolutely not.

The wildfire cannot take Pete. I won't let it.

I have to get him out *now.*

My shoes aren't dry, but I don't care. My clothes are, stiff from hanging on the line. I throw off Shook's clothes and pull on my shorts and shirt.

Should I wake Shook up?

Should I ask him to drive me into town now?

How far is it? Could I get there on one of the bikes?

Or the quad. The keys are right in the ignition. There are three jerry cans along the wall of the shed, so I take the one that's full of gas.

⟡ ⟡ ⟡

I find an apple on the counter, and a jar of peanuts. There is a slab of hard bread and some butter. I cut off a piece and slather it with butter. There is no fridge, but there is a cooler. I lift the lid and recoil. It stinks of fish. I find another jar with dried prunes and take a couple of those. I wrap the nuts and prunes in a square of waxed paper that's obviously been used many, many times before. I twist it and then hold it together with a little rubber band from a bowl full of them.

Otis follows me around as I look for something to write on. I find a piece of mail, unopened, the back blank.

Dear Shook,

Thank you for helping me.

I took your quad, but I'll leave it at the gas station.

I've taken some food too, but I'll come back someday to explain, and when I do, I will replace it.

Thank you for your hospitality.

Annie and Pete

When I see how I signed it, I want to rip it up, but there is nothing else to write on. So I leave it like that because I can't bear to cross out his name, and because I know he'd be thankful for the old man too.

Otis jumps onto the passenger seat while I'm sitting there, my fingers on the key, wondering if I'm really going to take this.

"Am I?" I say to the dog, or to the night, or to nothing at all.

Otis stares at me.

"You can't come," I say. "Off. Get off." When he doesn't, I give him a shove. He doesn't budge. "Get off!" I say as loudly as I can without yelling and waking up Shook. "Go. Go!"

He stares at me, his big tongue lolling out, panting.

What I want, more than pretty much anything else realistic, is for Otis to come with me. Even if it's only as far as the gas station. I can leave him there, with the quad, in some shade. I will leave him there, I tell myself. Shook will come for him. Which is the right thing to do, when I'm not going to do the actual right thing to do, which is to not take him in the first place. The next best thing, Gigi would call that.

I turn the key and the quad starts right away, much louder than our quads. I have to go quick or Shook will hear. I back out of the shed, reversing and turning so I can take a straight shot down the driveway. I grab Otis's collar so he doesn't fall off, but clearly he's used to the quad, because he leans into each curve as if he were born on one of these. I let go of his collar and put both hands on the handlebars and lean forward to see the road better, because only one headlight is working, and it must be pretty dirty, because I can hardly see at all.

It's not long before the dark sky starts to lighten, and I can see long orange wisps of cloud ribboned through the trees. We're speeding alongside the river now, and the rushing water looks like liquid silver.

It's good to be alive today! Pete shouts from behind me.

I don't look back. I know he's not there. And it's not good to be alive without him. Without Gigi. Without my mom.

Loss upon loss upon loss.

I have never thought that life was fair, but this is too much for one kid.

The sun is peeking up from the ridge to the east. I crest a small hill and see a stop sign reflecting in my one dim headlight. Otis stands up. He must know that we're getting close. I slow down, worried that he's going to fall. He jumps off and runs full-out toward the stop sign, dodging off to the right just before it.

"Otis!" I speed up. I can't lose Shook's dog too.

But as I get closer, I see that he's waiting for me at the junction.

HODGES CORNER STORE + GAS

GASOLINE

FISH BAIT

HUNTING LICENSES

ICE CREAM

PRINT SHOP

POST OFFICE

'N' MORE

This is it.

This is where it all becomes real.

This is where it ends.

This is where I tell.

The pay phone booth has no pay phone in it. That discovery unzips the last of my nerves, and I sit shaking, my chest hurting, waiting for the store to open at eight. I sit on a picnic table. It was painted orange at one point, which I can tell from the parts safe from the sun. The same orange as our tent. But the top is bleached white now and peeling. Otis sits at my side, panting. I circle the building and find a locked bathroom, but beside it is a tap that works. I drink out of cupped hands and then let Otis do the same. We go back to the table. I eat a few peanuts. Otis eats a few peanuts. We both watch the building.

I take out the diary and hold it in my hands. I do the opposite of opening it; I squeeze it shut. I put the rubber band from Shook's cabin around it. I dig in the lid of my pack and pull out a plastic bag and put it in there, and then I find my duct tape and I wrap it up.

I don't want to read what he wrote, yet I also do want to. So I don't. Not yet. Because you can't undo something after you've already done it.

There's a clock inside, above the register, and when I check it, it's not even seven, but as I turn to go back to the picnic table, the door opens and a big woman grabs me into a hug from behind.

"Oh, sweetheart!" She spins me around. Short, tubby, long gray hair flattened by sleep, a face full of smoker's wrinkles, like Gigi. "You're that girl, from the news last night. Where's your boyfriend, darling, he with you?"

"He's not my boyfriend."

"Your friend, then, hon, where is your friend?"

"Best friend."

"The news said . . ."

Why did the news say anything? We're not overdue yet.

Tell her.

This is it.

This is when you tell her what happened.

"This your dog?" She pats Otis's head as he butts her hip. "News didn't say anything about a dog."

"The news?"

"Honey, search and rescue has been out there looking for you and your boyfriend for two days."

"We're not late," I say. "We still have two days."

"What day do you think it is, darling?" The woman pulls me into the store and lets Otis come in with me. She turns on the coffeemaker and unwraps a Danish. "Eat this. Coffee will be just a minute. I'm going to call the sheriff's office. Search and rescue is way off track if you ended up here. Where's the boy?"

"Peter Alvarez Bonner."

"Where is he, darling?"

I haven't said it out loud, and now that I should, it seems entirely impossible. The Danish is limp in my hand. Otis grabs it, nearly biting my finger. The woman says hello to the dispatcher and starts explaining in a rush.

"Is the boy okay?" She covers the mouthpiece with a hand. "Is he hurt?"

Gigi is dead.

My mom is dead.

"Pete is dead."

"I'll call right back. I will. . . . Yes, I know. . . . Only a minute!" She hangs up the phone. "That can wait a minute, then." She hugs me again and doesn't let go. "You're sure? Absolutely sure?"

I nod, and then I start to cry.

The woman squeezes me tighter and starts to pray. It doesn't matter that Pete is an atheist. I'll take all the help I can get, and so will Pete. Even if he's dead.

"And may his soul rest in eternal peace, no matter where his earthly body is. Amen. Now I've really got to call them back," she says. "They didn't take kindly to me hanging up on them. But it's just fine to stop everything for a prayer." She goes back to the phone and makes the call. At some point, she hands the phone to me.

I tell the woman on the phone about our bright orange tent in the middle of the clearing by the creek about five miles north of the first cabin up from where I am. I say no, I'm not hurt. Which is a complete and utter lie.

✧ ✧ ✧

She says the sheriff will be there in half an hour. She says to stay put. She says she'll call my dad. And Pete's. She says I've been so strong. I did good. It's all over now.

"Oh, you are so brave. I just can't imagine. Thank goodness you knew what to do." She sits me behind the counter with her, even though there are tables near the coffee machine. I sit there with Otis Creek at my feet, clutching the diary.

"What you got there, honey?"

"Nothing."

"Your diary?"

I shake my head.

"That boy's diary?"

"No." I peel off the duct tape and take it out of the bag.

"It's pretty," Mrs. Hodges says.

"My mom gave it to me," I say. "Just before she died."

"Oh." The bell above the door rings. A customer, heading for the terrible coffee. "I bet that's been really special for you. A real comfort since her passing. I am sorry for your loss. Was that a long time ago?"

"When I was twelve."

"Oh dear," Mrs. Hodges says. "So hard to lose a mother at a young age. I'll pray for you."

The customer pays, then leaves. I get up and squeeze past Mrs. Hodges.

"I'm going to wait at the picnic table for the sheriff," I say. "I just need some fresh air."

◇ ◇ ◇

I flip to the pages Pete wrote.

Dear Annie,

If you are reading this, then I did die, right?

I'm okay with that.

Not the dying part, but the here-with-you part.

All that you need to know is that I love you.

I'm scared, Annie.

It's not your fault, and you have to know that's true because it could've been you.

Annie. Please. Listen.

I'm so sorry.

It's going to be hard, but you have to keep going on, because I am not going to be your excuse. Just think if it were you writing this letter. Think about what you would want for me.

What you want for me, I want so much for you too.

Consider this a contract between me and you for you to live both of our best lives, from this moment on.

I want for you to fill out the corners of your life for the two of us.

I miss you already.

And you will miss me.

Just don't let go. Don't let go of life.

Don't let go of me, or your mom, or Gigi.

But don't hold on too tight either.
I'm so sorry.
I love you.

xo
P.

PS. I never gave this journal to you, because when we were kids, I was afraid that it would make you more like her. I was going to give it to you now because I know that you're not like her in that way, even if the sky goes dark for you sometimes.

One Year Later

When we picked up his ashes from the crematorium, Everett took a scoop and put it into a little vial he wears around his neck. With ash on his fingertips and red-rimmed eyes, he gave me the rest to scatter.

"Some with his mother, okay?"

I put his ashes into a coffee tin and did that stop first. The hill behind his house where her ashes were scattered. Then I buckled the tin into the passenger seat of Pete's truck and drove to the first of our places.

I scattered some of his ashes at the agate beach, at the spot where he saw that big, golden rock that almost killed him.

I scattered some at the elementary school, where we met.

I scattered some at our tree house, or the remains of it.

And of course, Otis Creek, our own private world out of time and place.

Ugly Mug, the swimming pool, our fishing hole, and the bridge we liked to jump off of, into the river.

The front steps of his house. The front steps of my house. My backyard, his backyard, Preet's car—when she wasn't looking—and the corner where we had our lemonade stands.

I even found Ty and Paola at their rock and gem shop and tried to give them some of his ashes to take up to where they showed us the crystals, but they both shook their heads as I talked. They led me out the back door and into their truck with two quads strapped in the back and straight up to the crystal site, while Spencer barked and barked and Otis lay across my lap, yawning.

Just one more place to go.

Preet is with me, kitted out in borrowed clothes, my old backpack, and brand-new boots. I tried to talk her out of brand-new boots—hiking boots, no less—but she insisted. I have an entire package of moleskin. I imagine that we will use it all. I've described the terrain to her, but I don't think she gets it. I think she sees it like a movie. Flat, with all those dangerous features you'd see on a movie set on a mountain, with two kids in trouble and some wolves.

Otis is with me too. He hasn't left my side since that day we met by the river. After we stop in at Hodges Corner Store and endure rib-breaking hugs from Mrs. Hodges, we drive Pete's truck up to Shook's cabin. I want to give him a bag of groceries and apologize for taking his dog.

"It's no matter," he says as he pats Otis's now much bigger

head. "Wasn't never mine anyway, and I'm glad I don't have to feed him. I'm glad he brought you some comfort. I imagine he has?"

"We go everywhere together," I say. "He's my best friend," I add. It's true. Better to have a dog as a best friend than pity the person who would ever attempt to take Pete's place. "I'm thankful for him every single day, sir."

He puts out a hand for Preet to shake. She does, smiling.

"Who's this young lady you've brought with you?"

"Pete's girlfriend," I say.

"Oh, well now." His voice grows husky. "I'm very sorry for your loss, then."

"Thank you," Preet says.

"Would you walk us back to where you found me?" I ask. I want to cross the river and get cold again. I want to feel just a tiny bit of what I felt that day. Preet pales. I've told her about this part, prepared her for it. Told her it would be like a baptism.

The Church of the Unforgiving Wilderness.

"I could," he says. "But if you drive up three miles, there's a little suspension bridge I imagine would be a lot more comfortable. Just have to backtrack on the other side." He glances at Preet. Smooth skin. Perfect braids. Obviously brand-new bandana covering her head.

It's a hot day. The river is low.

I want to walk through it.

Preet will do whatever I tell her to. She's already told me that.

"I'd like to go back the way I came," I say. "It means a lot to me."

He shrugs. "Least take off your clothes when you cross," he says, rummaging under a cabinet for a couple of dirty black garbage bags. "No need to be soaking wet on the other side."

He walks us up to the spot and asks me what I'm doing with my truck.

"When are you coming back?"

"We're hiking through," I say. "We parked Preet's car at the other end of the trail. The truck is for you. The papers are signed. In the glove box. You just have to fill in your parts, if you want it."

Because words can't do the job I need them to. Words can't stake out the shape this old man took in making me who I am. The respite, just that one night, was so important. Most of all, I can't imagine life without Otis, and I have Shook to thank for him.

"You're giving me your truck?" His eyes go a little damp. "I'd say I don't need it, but you've seen mine."

"That's more of a chicken coop than a truck now. I'd like to give you this truck," I say. "Pete's truck. Please let me do this?"

"Let you? Well now." He shoves his hands in his pockets, and for a moment he looks like a tall, gangly teenager, with pink cheeks. And not a clue what to say. I can imagine Pete like this. Living here. Driving into town on an ATV. And I know for a fact that he can use the truck.

"How about this?" I hold out the keys. "How about I leave

it here until I come back to get it? The insurance is paid up. And it's got a mostly full tank of gas. And I even made this ramp. . . ."

I reach into the back and pull out a plank of wood that I covered in carpet.

"What the heck?"

I open the passenger door and set the ramp in place. His old dog knows exactly what it's for. He plods up it and onto the seat and curls into a greasy old ball.

"I am a grateful man, darling." He gives me an awkward hug.

"Annie," Preet says from the rocky edge of the river. "We should get going, right?"

"You should," Shook says. "But first I want to tell you a little funny thing. Last time you came, that first time, you met Shook. But that's not my real name."

"I didn't think so."

"I'm a Pete too," he says. "Peter Svendsen. It only occurred to me to tell you that after I heard about your friend."

For a few moments, I am hanging suspended in a small tear in the space-time continuum. This could've been Pete, decades from now. He might've looked like this old man. He could've lived like Shook, by a river, up a mountain, with grandkids coming and going. Off the grid, having outlived his wife and missing her still.

But not the rabbits on his belt.

Not his trapline.

Not how he'd vote, based on the stickers in the window of his dead truck.

This man is not Pete.

But he has a lot in common with him anyway.

Generous, forgiving, kind, capable, and happy to help.

"We're doing this, Preet!" I toss my pack into one of the garbage bags and put hers into the other. "Get as naked as you want."

I turn to make some joke about not watching us strip, but Shook is gone. I can see the blue of his baseball cap getting smaller and smaller down the trail. He isn't worried about us, not beyond us getting our things wet.

I strip down naked, and seeing me, Preet does the same.

We balance the plastic bags on our heads and step into the river.

"Oh my goodness!" Preet sucks in her breath. "We have to do it fast." She starts to pull away from me.

"No!" I hold her hand tight. "We have to do this so that we don't fall." The current pushes at our sides. "The rocks will be slippery. Small steps. That's why it's actually better to wear your boots, but we need them dry. I'll take the chance."

"We should've taken the bridge!" Preet yelps as the water covers her waist.

We make it across without falling. Preet dances and dances.

"I can't believe that we did that! I just crossed a river.

Naked!" She stops, facing the hot sun, and is quiet while I rearrange the packs.

"Come on," I finally say. "Let's get going."

Even though the forest is nearly all scorched to the west and south, I find the spot right away. Not because I suddenly know it in my bones, but because when search and rescue came to get Pete—Pete's *body*—they left everything else. The tent is exactly where I left it, weighed down by our things inside. The orange nylon is sun-faded, and the whole thing is streaked with dirt and still smells of smoke. I stand there, staring at it, willing Pete to be in there. Willing away the last year. Willing everything in fast rewind to that day when he brought pakora and falafel.

The wildfire shifted while it was still west of him, angling north and staying above him, but only by about five hundred feet. Although he always said it would be cool to die in a forest fire if he *had* to die, I know that was bluster. It would be terrifying to watch the flames get close. I'm glad that he didn't have to. When I see the tent, I am momentarily surprised that it's just a heap of flattened orange nylon, because despite my brain telling me otherwise, I think he should still be in there. This is the last place I saw him, after all. But life isn't magical, no matter how much I wish it were. There are no unicorns jumping over rainbows.

The poles are still in their slots, and even though the

rescuers cut the nylon to get Pete out, the poles still work to hold the tent up so that I can crawl in. My sleeping bag. His too. Sleeping mats. Empty coffee packets, chewed-through dried-milk bag, my dirty bowl, his dirty bowl, our sporks, and so much mouse poo. The notebook he'd been ripping pages from to make the origami unicorns. Pete's other shirt, a moldy, stiff puck on the floor. This is just trash. I thought I would want to bring home every ounce of it, right down to the actual garbage of the coffee packets. But I can't connect to these things that Pete and I brought here, that surrounded him when he died, that I walked away from. The things that I thought would be precious to me. Not dirty underwear and bowls peppered with mouse droppings.

Otis pushes in from behind me, but the tent with me and a rambunctious dog is far too small, so everything gets twisted and kicked around, and becomes even less precious, with Otis jumping and trying to catch the nylon in his teeth.

"Back up, Otis." There's the bottle of Gigi's THC tincture, hardly any worse for wear. I could pick it up and put it in my pocket. I could keep it. Use it. *No, Annie. You won't. You've been clean and sober ever since you were up here with me.* Sometimes I hear Pete, even now, whether I want to or not. "All right, all right," I say, grabbing on to Otis's collar. I untangle us from the tent and shimmy backward out into the sunshine, laughing as Otis steps all over me.

"Annie?" A hand on my shoulder. Surprised, I wrench away in one quick movement before I remember that Preet is with me. She's crying, but she's the one who asks if I'm okay.

"Yeah. I'm okay." I sit on the dirt and Otis climbs into my lap. Preet goes ahead and pulls the tent poles out, then turns the nylon upside down and shakes everything out. Now with just the faded orange material, she takes a pair of scissors from her backpack and starts cutting it into strips.

"What are you doing?"

"We're going to make prayer flags." She gets out a second pair of scissors and hands them to me. "Start cutting."

I should mind this, but I don't. This isn't her space, or her tent, or her story, even. Not up here, it isn't. It's her story from when I phoned her in India, but up here it's still all mine. Yet I start cutting up Pete's sleeping bag, glancing at what she's doing so my squares are about the same size as hers.

"Where did he die?" Preet holds a swath of the tent in her hands, as if holding orange flames, spilling down.

"In the tent."

"You said you dragged him into the clearing after," Preet says. "So they could find him. I want to know exactly where he died. Take me into the forest and show me. I want to see where we can hang the flags."

I look for the log that was like a bench. For the flattened space that might not be there anymore after a winter of rain and wind and snow and the forest going on without us. Then I see a tiny, glinting something on the ground ahead of me. It's the crystal from my tin of talismans!

"It was here," I say. "See?" I show her the crystal, and then I clear away more pine needles and pinecones and wind-fallen branches, looking for the rest of my little treasures. "Our tent was right here. We were trying to get some cover from the sun, and the ash too."

I don't find another talisman, just one of the bags we were using for water and a flavor packet for ramen noodles.

Preet shakes her head, eyes welling with tears.

"This isn't the right spot," she says. "Come on."

She leads me back to the edge of the clearing, where Otis is rolling in something likely very gross. "We'll string them between the two oak trees," she says. "I don't want them in the forest, if that's okay with you. It's dark in there, and too close to the burned trees."

"Okay," I say, because I'm not sure if this is meaningful to me at all, and if it is to her, then she can have it. Preet lies down under the big oak tree, on her back, looking up through the pines, and then she turns her head to look through the hopeful spring growth, the bright green leaves almost glowing in the sunlight. "This is the perfect spot. Out in the sunshine, where the trees are still green and living."

I don't even hesitate. I lie down beside her and offer my arm. She rests her head on it, and we both stare through the dancing, shimmering green. Otis curls against my side. All three of us fall asleep like that.

When I wake up, Preet is sewing the orange squares onto the seams of the tent, which she's cut into one long piece. She's written on many of them, but I don't want to know what they say.

"These are for you." She hands me a bunch, and I realize, looking around, that she's cut up the entire tent, plus Pete's shirt, which she must've washed in the creek, and the two sleeping bags. She's made enough ribbon that it could probably stretch all the way to the creek, and I wonder if that's her plan. She hands me the marker. "You can make a wish, or say a prayer for him. Or you don't have to do anything."

I put the first square in my lap and stare at it. I'm not going to do anything. These squares don't really matter. They don't mean anything more than the prayers I tried when Pete was dying. I don't believe in that kind of power, so this won't do anything for me. It works for Preet because she believes in her god, and dharma.

I don't believe in anything.

But yet I find myself putting the marker to the nylon and drawing the crystal I just found. I set it aside and pick up a square of his sleeping bag and draw a cube, for the pyrite. I draw the arrowhead on another, and for each talisman that I lost, I make a drawing on a square—the agate and the triangle of mica. They look like nothing at all, like some scribbles a toddler would make, but I know what they mean. I draw water, for the time we almost drowned. I draw the bridge we jumped off to get away from the man. The dam where they found my mom's body. The bathtub where he found his mom. A dog, for all the ones we walked. A TV for Gigi. Earth for Everett, and a big flower for my dad. A dahlia, like a firework.

I draw a star for Preet, a mountain for this place, flames for all the fire, and a heart for Otis, who is taking care of mine.

The last one I draw is a unicorn, jumping over the moon.

Of course.

The length of prayer flags is so long that I tie one end to a skinny pine tree at the edge of the burned forest, string it across the clearing where they found Pete, hook it on the little oak tree, and draw it all the way over to the big oak tree. I hand the end to Preet and catch a low branch and swing myself up. She passes up the ribbon, and I tie it above me with a double knot.

From up here, I can see across the creek and beyond the little grove on the other side. The view is what Pete called "suntacular." The sun is starting to set, so the light is illuminating only one side of everything. There is a dark side, and there is a light side. There is a world without Pete, and there is a world with Pete, even now.

I hold the flags on this end tight in my fist. I might not believe enough to pray, but these are talismans, like the ones I lost. They're all here somewhere, and now these flags will be too, until the elements decide it's time to take them, like they took Pete. I rest my forehead against the tree trunk, my fist closed so tight around the cloth that my fingers feel numb.

Tears wet my cheeks, which are so dirty that when the tears fall and land on my other arm, they are little dark splotches.

Otis puts his paws on the trunk below, whining. My heart guard can't get up to me.

You left me, Pete.

That was never part of the deal.

I am so sorry that I couldn't save you.

I take the marker from my pocket and turn over the flag with the unicorn on it.

I'm sorry, I write.

I write the same thing on the back of the rest of the flags in my hand.

I'm sorry.

I'm sorry.

I'm sorry.

I'm sorry.

After we scatter the last of his ashes in the clearing, neither of us wants to sleep. I don't want to sleep anywhere nearby even, so as it gets dark, we switch on our headlamps and I take Preet's hand and we make our way into the forest, heading for the hot spring, with my GPS fully charged and topographical maps in my pack and on my phone, which I can always charge up with my new solar-powered power bank. Coyotes yip in the distance. Otis barks back, and they wisely fall silent.

"I'm really afraid," Preet says. "But I trust you."

This was my best hope for Pete, at the end.

That even though he was really afraid, he trusted me.

✧ ✧ ✧

After the hike, when we finally get to where we left Preet's car, I put my hand on the roof. Warm from days of sunshine, cute and compact. Like Preet.

"Barely two hours from civilization!" She dumps her pack into the trunk and stands by, waiting for me to put mine in too. Otis is normally the first one into any car, but he's sticking by my side, obviously clued in to the fact that I have no intention of getting into the car. "Come on, let's go. Ice cream sandwiches are in our very near future, my dear."

"I'm not coming with you, Preet." When she opens her mouth to protest, I hold up my hands. "Wait, wait. Just let me talk."

But what can I say, really? And why didn't I come up with something sooner? All this time, hiking and thinking, and not once did I try to sort out what this moment might look like. I want to say everything to her, but I can't. I just can't.

"Would you take me up to the PNT? I want to hike back to Shook's."

"Haven't you had enough?"

"I never get tired of being out here, Preet."

"Really?" She shakes her head and crosses her arms, which she does only when she's preparing to win an argument, which she'll probably still do in the courtroom in front of the jury when she becomes a lawyer. This is not Preet's place. She doesn't like any of this. The bugs, the dirt, the unpredictable weather, sleeping on a mat on the ground, eating reconstituted vegetarian lasagna with a spork out of a titanium pot. She can't understand.

"You can't tell me that you still want to be out here, after everything?"

"I do." I pull her into a hug. "Unfold your arms and hug me back."

"I worry about you," she says.

"So do I." I kiss her cheek, then the other.

"I don't love you just because Pete loved you," she says. "Although that is what it was in the beginning, when you hated me. And don't insult my intelligence by claiming that you didn't hate me. I know how it was for you."

"Maybe there was a little bit of hate," I say. "But you don't know how it was for me. For me and Pete. Since we were little."

"Well, I love you, Annie."

I never thought about loving her. She belonged to Pete. She was the beautiful, wonderful thing that was taking him away from me. But I trusted him. So if he loved her . . .

I cannot believe that it took me this long to get to this moment.

So if he loved her, then it's okay for me to love her too. Especially now. I sweep Preet into another hug, this one tight and messy as we both cry all over each other's shoulders and Otis bumps his dirty head against our legs, worried for both of us.

"I love you too, Preet!" I pull away and hold her at arm's length. "I absolutely love you! Now drive me up the road ten miles and drop me off at the PNT and go get yourself an ice cream sandwich!"

"You're crazy, Annie," Preet says as she gets into the car.

"I come by it naturally."

"I didn't mean your mom," she says. "You know that, right?"

"It's okay." I hold up a hand. "Better the devil you know."

"Honestly, though, you shouldn't be out here alone. What is out there? This is ridiculous. Come home with me, please? What am I supposed to tell your dad?"

"Tell him that I'm not ready," I say. "This forest? The wilderness? The mountains and the ocean and rivers and all the dense quiet in between? This is where I need to be right now."

For a moment, Preet doesn't say anything, and then her shoulders slump, and I know she isn't going to argue anymore.

"Tell him I'll send him letters. Folded into origami unicorns. Or my sad attempt at unicorns. Pete must've shown me a hundred times, but mine still look like pieces of paper folded into messy folded-up pieces of paper. When they come, just know that they're unicorn heads."

"You'll send me some too?" Preet smiles.

"You too," I say. "I already have the square paper, and I already have the envelopes, and I already have the stamps. I'm not going away, Preet. I promise. I'm just *going.*"

Preet drops me off ten miles up the road at the trailhead to the Pacific Northwest Trail that Pete and I didn't even get close to, and then she drives away slowly, keeping me in sight in the rearview mirror as long as she can, just in case I change my mind and decide to go with her. I have to wait until she crosses the first cattle guard and takes the corner, because I don't want her to see that I'm not getting on the trail to go see Shook. I know I'll see him again, but not just yet.

Instead, I stay on the road and carry on north, with Otis at my heels. When I hear a logging truck behind me, I stick out my thumb, and it stops so Otis and I can climb up into the cab. While Preet was asleep the night before, I scrolled up the topo maps until I found the nearest train tracks west to east. Otis and I are going to hop a train going east to I don't know where.

Pete will be with us, even if he isn't. Just like Gigi, and my mom too. It will be crowded with all of us, but not so crowded that I can't run to catch a train, with my dog jumping up behind me. Not so crowded that we can't all sit there and watch the mountains rush by, with wildfire smoke in the distance.